The Fairy Tale Friend

Other Crossway Books
by Marcia Hoehne

THE ADVENTURES OF JENNA V.
A Place of My Own
A Pocket in My Heart

The Fairy Tale Friend

THE ADVENTURES OF JENNA V.

Marcia Hoehne

CROSSWAY BOOKS • WHEATON, ILLINOIS
A DIVISION OF GOOD NEWS PUBLISHERS

The Fairy Tale Friend

Copyright © 1994 by Marcia Hoehne

Published by Crossway Books
          a division of Good News Publishers
          1300 Crescent Street
          Wheaton, Illinois 60187

Cover illustration: Joy Dunn Keenan

Art Direction/Design: Mark Schramm

First printing 1994

Printed in the United States of America

Library of Congress Cataloging-in-Publication Data
Hoehne, Marcia, 1951-
    The fairy tale friend / Marcia Hoehne.
    p.   cm.—(Adventures of Jenna V. series: bk.3)
    Summary: When eleven-year-old Jenna and her family visit her grandparents at the lake, she strikes up a friendship with the frail young woman next door.
    1. Death—Fiction. [1. Friendship—Fiction. 2. Family Fiction. 3. Christian life—Fiction.] I. Title. II. Series: Hoehne, Marcia, 1951- Adventures of Jenna V. series: bk. 3.
PZ7.H667Fai 1994   [Fic]—dc20   94-25771
ISBN 0-89107-813-4

02		01		00		99		98		97		96		95		94
15	14	13	12	11	10	9	8	7	6	5	4	3	2	1

For Keith,
who let me borrow his words—
and his Superman cape

Contents

❧ **1** ❧

Woman in the White Dress

"**A**RE WE THERE YET, DAD?" PETER Vander Giffin asked for the several-hundredth time.

"Yes," Dad declared, steering the station wagon slowly up the narrow gravel road. "Yes, *now* we are *finally* there. Grandma and Grandpa's cottage should be just around the bend. We are now officially Up North."

Eleven-year-old Jenna wiggled with excitement. A whole vacation at Grandma and Grandpa Schellenburg's new cottage on the lake! She'd miss her friends, especially her best friend Kate, but she was also glad to be Up North. After all, Up North was where everybody went. Everybody had a cottage on a lake with a name like Long Lake or Pine Lake, or sometimes a distinctive name like White Potato Lake. Jenna giggled to herself, wondering if there was a Sweet Potato Lake too.

"Dad, where does Up North start?" asked Peter.

"Does the cottage look be-sactly like Sleeping Beauty's cottage?" queried Maria.

"What's the name of Grandma and Grandpa's lake?" Jenna put in.

But she never got an answer. Around the next bend was not Grandma and Grandpa's cottage. Around the next bend was a sight that drove everything else from her mind and made six-year-old Maria practically jump across her lap to reach the window, straining against her seat belt, shrieking her question into Jenna's ear.

"Who is that beautiful princess?"

At the arched stone entryway of a tiny cottage stood a slender, dark-haired young woman in a flowing white dress. The stucco walls of the cottage were a surprising but peaceful soft blue. A rounded alcove, which on a taller house would have been a tower, curved out from its left side. As their car passed the cottage, the woman raised one hand to her forehead to brush a curl away or to shade her eyes from the low sun.

The car slowed abruptly.

"Faster, Dad," urged Peter.

"Easy, son. I can't climb up Mom's tail pipe, you know."

Mom, driving the car ahead, must be as surprised as she was, Jenna thought. Certainly Lia and Cara, riding with her, had clamored for her to slow down so they could see the cottage and the girl.

The girl's—the *woman's*—filmy dress swayed in the wind, and her wavy hair blew in a cloud around her face. Her tiny cottage surrounded by pines belonged by the sea, Jenna thought, although she had never seen the sea. In the yard a small sign swung from a pole. Jenna saw the picture on it. There were no words on the small wooden plaque, only a painting of a blue flower, maybe a rose.

"Hey, quite some babe," David observed. David was fifteen and had recently turned his attention from sports long enough to discover girls.

"And a good eight years older than you, I'd guess," Dad said dryly.

"Let's get going," Peter moaned.

"Now we're not going slow only to sightsee," Dad pointed out. "Mom's taking it easy because the gravel's sharp here. We don't want to end up with a punctured tire."

The two cars crawled past the little cottage, and soon a blacktopped drive branched out from the gravel road. Mom turned onto it, then Dad. The driveway wound in a semicircle to an open garage, which was topped by a two-story lustrous honey-bronze house with a steeply slanted roof. A railing zigzagged all around the deck and landings and stairwells. The front wall of the house was almost completely glass. To Jenna, the house looked like a ship.

"Grandma and Grandpa!" Peter and Maria cried at the same time. It seemed they flew right over the other occupants of the car, leaving Dad, David, Jenna, and Sherry behind in a cloud of dust. Jenna looked at Sherry, her newly-adopted same-age sister, and rolled her eyes. Sherry brushed her blonde hair away from her face and answered with a giggle and a smile.

Jenna was eager to see her grandparents too, and she was grateful to finally pile out of the car and stretch and let the lake breeze cool her limbs. She pushed her wiry hair off the back of her neck and thought of the young woman in white with her dark hair blowing. She pushed at her own dark hair again, hoping the wind might catch it.

"Oh, what beautiful scenery," Lia cried, holding her arms out and whirling in delight. Her long, blonde hair flared out like graceful streamers. The skirt of her sun dress clung to her legs on one side and swung out like a bell on the other. Again Jenna thought of the young woman in the long windblown dress down the road.

"Lia's right," Jenna heard Mom say in a low voice to Dad.

She turned to see how Mom looked in the

wind. Mom flicked her thick rope of a braid over one shoulder. Dark tendrils of hair danced around her face. Dad's blond curly hair bounced as it blew flat in one spot, then another, then another, and sprang up again.

"I'd love to have devotions out here, Mark," Mom continued. "I didn't know it would be this gorgeous."

"Sherry, my newest grandchild," Jenna heard Grandma saying behind her. "Well, I think you've grown since last month. I'll have to take you down the road to meet old Mrs. Barber. I've been telling her about my new granddaughter, but I don't think she understands you're eleven years old. I'm afraid she thinks Linda had another baby!"

Jenna gazed at the lake, which was dotted with foamy whitecaps and spread bluer and bluer to the sharp line of the horizon. Above, the sky and clouds swirled together in marbled blues, grays, and whites. The complete picture was so soft, cool, and peaceful it made Jenna want to run down to the shore and plunge right in—whether into the lake or the sky, she wasn't sure.

"We get some mighty fine sunrises on the water." A man's familiar voice spoke behind her.

"Hi, Grandpa." Jenna turned and smiled. He wasn't much taller than she was anymore, and his hair had gone grayer than she'd realized. But his craggy face and twinkling blue eyes hadn't changed.

"Bet a person could bring a note pad out here, sit down, and have themselves a fine challenge describing what they see."

Jenna grinned.

"Unless you're the type that can't get out of the sack in the morning."

Jenna wasn't sure, but since this was vacation and she was surrounded by beauty, why not try? "I can do it."

"Atta girl." Grandpa patted her shoulder. "Well, looks like everybody's meandering inside. Come on up; Grandma's got a spread waiting, you know."

"You mean food?" Jenna's stomach suddenly contracted with hunger. "Does she have the nut bread she always buys? And crunchy peanut butter?" This was what Grandma always served when the family arrived at her house for a stay. Jenna's knees grew weak at the remembered aroma of the nut bread.

"Better come on up and check it out." Grandpa turned toward the house, but not before he let Jenna see the twinkle in his eyes.

Jenna started eagerly forward, wanting to be inside with everyone, wanting to see the house, which was much bigger than she'd expected a cottage to be. But it was the very size of the house that made her think again of the tiny cottage next door. She craned her neck, trying to catch a glimpse of blue siding or a slope of gray roof through the towering trees, and wondered once again who the woman in the white dress could be.

❦ 2 ❦

The Beautiful Hermitess

*G*RANDMA'S SPREAD WAS MORE THAN peanut butter and nut bread. She'd lapped alternating slices of cheese and sausage spiral-fashion on a platter. There were carrot and celery sticks, green grapes and peaches, and lemonade. Mom set Tyler in his highchair and put Ben in his booster seat. Though they couldn't all sit at the table, the Vander Giffins clasped hands around it to pray before they ate.

Jenna was amazed to notice that they stood or sat in the same order they always did at home: Jenna, David, Dad, Maria, Cara, Peter, Lia, Tyler, Mom, Ben, Sherry, and back to Jenna.

"Lord," Dad prayed, "we thank You for blessings—homes and families, food and safe travel, health and work, and vacations. For Your love and care we are truly grateful. Amen."

"A-men," everybody said.

Jenna joined those sitting at the table, while others loaded their plates and wandered off in twos or threes to sit in the great room or to step through the sliding doors onto the deck.

"They can go wherever they want," Grandma reassured Mom with a wave of her hand. "We furnished the house with children in mind."

As Grandma and Grandpa approached the table, it struck Jenna that they hadn't taken part in the prayer. A troubled feeling rose in her. Her family had been praying for a long time that Grandma and Grandpa Schellenburg would become Christians. She guessed it hadn't happened yet. She guessed prayers still made Grandma and Grandpa uncomfortable. These thoughts were erased from her mind by a question from Maria.

"Grandma, who's the beautiful princess next door?"

Jenna stopped spreading crunchy peanut butter on nut bread and looked up at Grandma expectantly.

"Oh." Grandma smiled. Her smile made her look a lot like Mom even though her hair was short and silvery instead of dark and long. She sipped coffee while leaning against the wall next to the table since all the chairs were filled. "So you've already seen Maralissa."

"Mara—" Jenna wanted to pronounce all the syllables she thought she'd heard. "Mare—ah—*liss*—ah?"

"Yes, isn't that quite the name? Maralissa Rose."

"Maralissa Rose?" Jenna wondered if people could die of too much beauty.

"Mala—rissa Rose what?" Maria asked.

"Maralissa Rose. Rose is her last name," Grandma said.

Jenna sighed dreamily.

"Beautiful hermit is more like it." Grandpa Schellenburg, sitting across the table from Jenna, washed down a bite of sandwich with a slurp of coffee. "Little standoffish if you ask me."

"Grandpa!" Cara scolded, licking peanut butter from her teeth, chin, and knuckles. "A hermit is a little old man!"

"Hermitess then. A beautiful hermitess," Lia pronounced in a gushy voice. Jenna, Mom, and Grandma laughed.

"Hermitess? Isn't that some President's house?" The bouncy rhythm in Grandpa's voice and the mad winking of his eyes told Jenna he was making a joke.

"That's Hermitage, Grandpa," David called from his cross-legged position on the great room rug. "Andrew Jackson named his house the Hermitage."

"Ahh," Grandpa said knowingly. "Say, that's another thing that Mara—whosits did, you know. Named that little cabin."

Jenna rose half out of her chair. "She named it! Named it what?" she implored, directing her question to Grandma.

"She calls it Bluerose Cottage. Had a sign made for out front and everything. No words on it though. Just a blue rose." Tucking her left arm around her own still-slender waist, Grandma sipped her coffee.

"Where'd you ever find that out anyway?" Grandpa asked Grandma. "It's not as if she talks to anybody."

"Oh, Stan, I don't know why you think that's so strange. We're new up here too, and most of the neighbors mind their own business. I ran into her at the store once or twice. When I spoke to her, she was real pleasant."

"Hmph," said Grandpa.

"She reminds me of Emily Dickinson." Lia wrinkled her nose at a piece of mangled cheese Tyler tossed from his highchair tray. "There was a picture of her in my English book. She wore white dresses and wrote poetry and died young."

"And hid in her house," said Grandpa.

"At least she died sort of young," Lia corrected herself. "I guess she was in her fifties. Well, maybe she was sort of old after all."

"Whoa," said Grandpa.

Grandma laughed. "Watch your step, young lady. She was just the right age. Right, Stan?"

Grandma tipped her head to catch Grandpa's eyes and then smoothed her hair with the same gesture Mom used—a hooking motion with the pinkie to catch the stray curl. Her blue eyes were the same as Mom's too, when they took on that young, teasing light. Jenna wondered if this was the kind of thing poets noticed.

"I wonder if Maralissa writes poetry," Jenna mused.

"I hate to be a wet blanket," Mom said, "but I'd feel better if we changed the subject. I don't know if I'd want to be talked about as much as we've talked about Maralissa." She wiped Tyler's face, hands, and even the blond curls on his forehead. She let him out of his highchair, and he ran screeching as if freed from prison.

Jenna sighed. She wondered why the big talkers like Lia always got to say whatever they wanted and when she, quiet Jenna, said something, it often seemed she had spoken out of turn. It was not the first time she'd felt this way, and she meant to take it up with the Lord soon.

Still, she partly agreed with Mom. For the first time she wondered how Maralissa had felt about the Vander Giffins. What had she thought when she'd stood outside Bluerose Cottage, watching two station wagons come crawling up her road, eleven heads hanging out the open windows, gawking?

Bluerose Cottage.

Jenna thought fleetingly of the Beautiful Gate, the little house they'd had in the back yard at home. Had it really been almost a year since they'd built it?

An idea mounted inside her. "Grandma?" Her voice quavered. She shouldn't have spoken yet. She should have waited to get Grandma alone, if that was possible.

Grandma had already gone to the kitchen with plates and leftovers. "What?" she called.

Jenna couldn't answer now, so she scooped up some glasses and the fruit bowl and headed for the kitchen.

"She is definitely up to something," she heard Cara say confidingly to Lia.

"Jenna's talking in her wiggle voice," Maria announced. "She must have an idea."

"Oh, what would you know about it?" Cara snapped at Maria. Without turning around, Jenna heard Cara flounce into the great room.

Pushing the fruit bowl into the refrigerator, setting the glasses in the sink, Jenna wanted to know why she couldn't say one word without her family deciding she must have a plot to change the world. Or were they so sure she would say something stupid that they were hanging around to get their laugh? She was definitely going to talk to Jesus about this shaky-voice business immediately.

"Did you call me?" Grandma asked her. "Now you know you don't have to work here, at least not tonight. I'm just going to quick load the dishwasher."

"You *have* one?"

"You bet." Grandma slid the door open to show her.

Jenna smiled into its depths. At her house the desire for a dishwasher was a major issue, and she'd just gotten another idea.

"Hey, you guys, come here and see Grandma's dishwasher."

Three squealing girls flew across the open space between the dining room and kitchen.

"I wonder if we're getting this kind," Lia said.

"How much have we got saved up again?" Cara asked.

"I get to push the button," said Maria.

Jenna took Grandma aside. A feeling of foolishness stabbed her, but she made herself ask. "Grandma, can I name your cottage?"

Grandma looked startled and then studied her. "You mean a name we would really use? Well, I don't know. That seems kind of like putting your nose in the air. We're just everyday people."

"Oh, but it's not," Jenna rushed on, keeping her voice low. "It kind of shows that the house is special to you—" Jenna stopped, uncertain how to say what she meant. "If you don't like the name, or if Grandpa doesn't, you don't have to use it. But I hope—"

"But you hope we would really call the house the name you pick?"

Jenna nodded. She was barely aware of the muffled male voices coming from the deck behind them, of the three girls running from the kitchen and pounding up the stairs.

"And get a sign too, I suppose?"

Jenna smiled.

Grandma smiled back. "Okay. You name the house, and if the name catches on, we'll get a sign. As long as nobody else gets upset that *they* couldn't name the house. If I end up running a Name-Grandma-and-Grandpa-Schellenburg's-Cottage Contest, I'll have to take nineteen entries, and I'll end up hurting eighteen sets of feelings. Do you see what I mean?"

Jenna ran quickly through a mental list of her ten Schellenburg cousins. "A lot of them are too young."

"Still, it could turn out to be trouble."

Jenna nodded. "Can I see the whole house? I mean I'll go inside and outside around the yard to get ideas for what to name it—"

"Jenna!" Maria cried. There was a tremendous clatter of footsteps down the stairs, and Maria hopped into the great room. "Come upstairs! You've just got to see what's up there. You've never seen anything like it in your entire Christian life!"

❦ 3 ❦

Upstairs at the Cottage

JENNA LAUGHED AND HURRIED toward the stairs. Maria must have been listening to the adults again.

Grandma let out a nervous giggle, and her footsteps followed Jenna across the great room. "Oh, you'll love the dorm. We built it with all of you kids in mind."

Maria pounded up the carpeted stairs, and Jenna ran after her. Even Grandma came behind at a trot.

"This way, Bob or Mike or Deb could bring their kids up too, and there's plenty of room for all of you."

Jenna knew that a dorm was where college kids lived—a building with a lot of separate bedrooms. She tripped on a step in excitement. Was the second floor of this shiplike house filled with individual bedrooms? Would hers look out on the pearly clouds and wrinkly lake on the east end, or maybe nest her in the high branches of the evergreens on the west?

Reaching the landing with a thump, Maria dodged suddenly to the right. Jenna, barreling behind, nearly crashed into Lia, who tossed her blonde hair and looked over her shoulder at Jenna with disdain.

"Now, it's actually divided into two parts." Grandma appeared at the head of the stairs, puffing slightly. "The left half can be for the boys this time, and the right for the girls. And this floor has a bathroom to itself." Grandma smiled broadly. "You're going to have so much fun up here. Just like a slumber party."

Jenna wandered around as Grandma pointed things out. There weren't separate bedrooms at all, but two good-sized lofts, one larger than the other. The smaller one, meant for the boys, overlooked the great room and was separated from it and from the stairwell by high railings rather than walls. The glossy, curving slats of honey-colored wood slid coolly under Jenna's fingers. Four cots stood here in a row.

The larger loft was an actual room, with two screened windows that made Jenna feel she could reach out and swing in the trees. Leafy branches rustled in the wind, and the evergreen boughs dipped up and down like carousel ponies. Birds twittered. A mourning dove cooed. On the plush cinnamon-colored carpet, five cots with puffy pillows waited. The assorted blankets were turned down at one corner, showing just a bit of crisp, smooth sheet.

"Well, thank you, Grandma. I think we'll settle in." Lia waved one hand free from its arms-crossed position on her chest. As Grandma headed down the stairs, Lia planted her hands on her hips and looked around the room. "This is not a dorm. This is a ward."

"I love it," Jenna said.

Lia groaned elaborately. "Of course *you* love it. Whatever I say or think or do, you do the opposite."

"I love it too," Maria asserted, chin high.

"Oh fine, let's choose sides," Lia huffed.

Cara browsed along the walls as if she were visiting an art gallery. She was practicing her Lia gestures—arms akimbo, though they weren't model-slim enough; hair flouncing, though it wasn't long and blonde enough—while wearing a studied frown. She turned to give her verdict. "I agree with Lia."

"Surprise, surprise," Lia muttered.

"But how can you not like it?" Jenna hurried to one of the windows, hoping to feel the breeze, but the loft faced opposite the lake. Instead she heard the rustling and whistling of wind and leaves again, loving these sounds that were not noise. A flock of little gray-brown birds swooped from branch to branch as if swinging on tiny Tarzan vines. "Do you know what God is showing you out this window, Lia?" she said bravely. "He's showing you all the different greens He made."

Jenna turned to Lia in time to see a flash of recognition cross her face. Lia, after all, was a painter. She might have been pouting about not having a private studio on the glass side of the house. But if anyone could appreciate the view here—the controlled riot of blue-greens, apple-greens, olive-greens, and white-veined greens, the textures of bark, needles, and grass—Lia could.

Lia's face had closed again, but Jenna risked another question. "Doesn't it seem funny that *I* would like this big room that's going to have everybody in it, and *you* don't?"

"Hilarious," said Lia.

Jenna turned back to the window. Maybe it wasn't so funny. She had thought Lia was the sociable type, always the laughing, witty center of any group. Lia adored drama and therefore thrived on an audience, and she was the oldest girl here. Why wasn't she pirouetting the length of the room, throwing the windows wide open, crooning big-sisterly wisdom with her hands cupped about their shoulders, making Jenna feel dull just by being herself? It seemed Lia had changed.

But she saw what I meant when I told her about all

the greens, Jenna thought. A light feeling rose in Jenna. She didn't really think about the feeling, as if it were a bubble that too much prodding might burst. But at that moment she felt glad to be Jenna; she felt glad to be dark-haired in contrast to Lia's blonde, and she even wondered if she might be more than just quiet Jenna—if she could find her way out of herself to talk.

Two muffled thuds shook her from her thoughts. For a second she strained to see above the trees, looking for lightning to go with the thunder, but the thuds rose up the stairs and exploded onto the landing.

"Superman!" cried Ben, charging into the girls' room.

"Hey cool, a basketball court," came David's new young-man's voice. "All I need is masking tape for the center line and the free-throw stripes and—aaggh, a wrestling ring!" he hollered, followed by a tremendous crash.

"Ha-ha, I'm gonna wrestle you," Peter yelled.

"Hey, your name may be David, but you fall like Goliath," Cara called from the girls' loft. Then she put her hands on her hips.

Lia stalked to the doorway between the two lofts. Curious, Jenna followed.

"With a thud like that," Lia pronounced, "you are going to break that loft right off, and it will fall plummeting to the great room floor."

David laughed, but Peter's eyes opened wide, and he rolled off of David's chest.

"And you will land on your seat in the wood stove."

"Oh, lighten up." David made a disgusted face.

"Superman!" Ben leaped past the knot of people in the doorway, the bath towel pinned around his neck flying behind him. He somersaulted across the boys' loft until his feet hit the railing. Then, shrieking, he dragged himself away, all waving arms and legs and twisted towel. "I'll fall through! I can't sleep up here!"

"Ben." David sat up. "The bars are way too narrow to fall through. You can't fall out, just like you couldn't fall between the bars of your crib when you were a baby."

Cara began to giggle hysterically. "That's what this whole thing is, a crib for the boys! Look at it. The walls on the ends are like the head and the foot, and then there are the side rails all the way down the side!"

All the girls exploded with laughter.

"The boys are in a crib," sang Maria.

"In a cage," burbled Cara.

"In the zooooo," Jenna yodeled, surprising herself.

"And I'm my brothers' keeper," Lia choked. "The zoo keeper."

Doubled over, Jenna laughed so hard she couldn't inhale.

"That does it." David jumped to his feet and flew at them.

"Children!"

David sprawled on the landing with another Goliath-like boom. Jenna looked down the stairs to see her parents standing at the bottom.

"What has gotten into you?" Mom asked.

"Your grandparents," Dad said, climbing the stairs, "built this for your comfort and pleasure. Thanks and normal use are welcome. Criticism, ungratefulness, and combat are not." He reached the landing and swept his children with a brown-eyed gaze. "Understand?"

Jenna nodded. Around her, other heads bobbed amid murmurs of "okay" and "yes, Dad." She wondered if Grandma and Grandpa thought they didn't like the loft. Jenna was sure everyone did, even Lia and Cara, who seemed to have to *think up* reasons to be unhappy. She hoped Grandma and Grandpa knew that.

Jenna strolled back into the girls' loft as the others began to wander away. She felt the small stirrings of a quiet person creeping up on her right, and though it might have been Maria, she somehow knew it was Sherry.

"You missed the big scene," Jenna said.

"Nobody missed it," Sherry answered, and they exchanged small smiles.

"So, how do you like the loft?" Jenna asked.

"I think . . ." Sherry paused, and Jenna turned to look at her. "I think it looks just like the nursery in Peter Pan."

Jenna gave her a slow, broad smile. She was going to like having Sherry for a sister. "I think you should tell that to Lia. And offer her a chance to play the part of Wendy."

❧

Walking around the outside of the cottage at dusk, Jenna discovered it was built into the side of a hill. She climbed toward the setting sun, toward the grove of trees both leafed and evergreen that Maria had named Mixed-Up Forest. The railed stairs that traveled up the side of the house seemed to move with her, like a train on a parallel track.

"Aren't there an awful lot of steps here for you?" Mom had asked Grandma a little while ago. Jenna, Grandma, and Mom stood on the deck looking down on the blacktopped driveway and the game of Keep Away that Jenna hadn't wanted to join. "Can Dad handle all this climbing?"

"Nonsense," Grandma had returned. "I don't plan to worry about all that for twenty years yet. Besides, we can always enter on the garage level.

There's a door right into the basement, and from there it's just one flight up."

Now, as Jenna continued her climb, she saw that the yard buckled and dipped in many places. Grass was sparse. A few boulders offered seats, if one didn't mind sitting on a boulder. Hauling her book bag, Jenna watched her feet for the last few yards. Then she rounded the corner of the house and sank gratefully into the greener, longer grass that thrived in its shade. She misted herself with mosquito spray and opened her Bible. She was somewhere in Luke, she knew, but the bookmark was missing.

At the beginning of July, Dad had challenged David, Lia, Jenna, and Sherry to a Bible-reading program. For each chapter they read they would be paid a dime, and they could earn up to two dollars and fifty cents a week. "Any more than that will break the bank," Dad had said, raising his hands in a shrug.

"And encourage speed reading," David observed.

"I'll ask from time to time what you've been reading," Dad had concluded. "But as long as there are no tricks like reading the same chapter over and over, you're on the honor system."

Jenna had started with Luke because she wanted to read about the birth of Jesus. She hadn't been reading fast. Though it was the seventeenth of the month, she was just about to earn her first dollar. She paged to Luke 10 and the story of the Good Samaritan.

Lord, first I want to ask if You'll help me name the cottage, Jenna prayed. *And, oh yes, why is it that my voice quivers whenever I have an idea? I would like to have better self-control. And how come other people get to talk, but when I talk, it's time to change the subject?*

Jenna's head snapped up. Once more she strained to see through the stand of trees that curved from west to south, hiding Bluerose Cottage from her. Because, of course, the subject that had been changed was Maralissa.

Did she dare go over there?

Anxiety swooped across her stomach. It was getting too dark to try to go through the trees. She didn't know what the ground would be like. And she knew her parents wouldn't want her walking along the narrow gravel road at dusk to call on a stranger. Buried under these thoughts was a feeling she didn't want to admit—she was scared. If she met the fairy-tale woman, what would she say?

Probably nothing, or at least nothing sensible, and her fantasy would be ruined. And probably Lia would step in and laugh her ripply laugh and say all the things Jenna should have, and Lia and Maralissa would forever after spend their days playing tag in the trees and taming the birds and chipmunks like a couple of wood nymphs.

I'll just read the Bible now, Lord, Jenna thought.

In the story, a teacher of the Law was stating the two great commandments to Jesus. "Love the Lord your God with all your heart, with all your soul, with all your strength, and with all your mind," and "Love your neighbor as yourself."

Another shiver ran through Jenna, and she looked toward the trees automatically. Back to the Bible.

"You are right," was Jesus' reply. "Do this and you will live."

But the teacher of the Law—Jenna gasped. She saw the words that were coming, and she knew how her voice would warble if she read them aloud.

But the teacher of the Law asked Jesus—

Jenna looked hard at the trees this time, wanting beams from her eyes to part the branches. But the greens were shutting down to gray now. Soon they'd be black. Lights were going to wink on, and grown-up voices would call. Feet would scamper up the wooden stairs to the door.

Jenna let her Bible fall into her lap and, with the teacher of the Law, spoke his words.

"Who is my neighbor?"

❧ 4 ❧

Lost and Found Words

JT WAS LATE WHEN THE GIGGLES finally faded out of the loft that night, but still Jenna poked her head up when her watch beeped at 5:15 on Saturday morning. Creeping on all fours between her bunk and Sherry's, she gave in to the urge to sink face down into the carpet. It still smelled new, like clean plastic. She shook herself, got up, and pulled a pair of shorts on under her long T-shirt.

Outside, the world looked like black and white TV, but the birds chattered expectantly. *They know about the sun*, Jenna thought, *and they're telling us so. Or do they think they're calling it?* She went down the wooden steps barefoot, and at the bottom tossed her sandals onto the blacktop and stepped into them. The sky ahead was still washed in a dusky lavender, but on the necklace of sand along the lake a gray-haired man was already sitting.

"Made 'er up, I see," Grandpa said.

"Yup," Jenna answered proudly. Actually, she had hoped to beat him to the beach.

"You got some backbone. Most kids today wouldn't bother. Too much privilege makes not enough purpose."

Jenna wasn't sure what he meant, but she didn't want a lecture on kids today. "Did you bring a notebook, Grandpa?" She would have liked to ask if he kept a journal, but she felt embarrassed wording it that way.

"Nah—I'm not clever with words. I'd sooner just soak it in. But I appreciate those who are." He jerked his head toward her and flashed her a hint of a smile.

The horizon began to light up, and the gray-lavender color climbed away. It was a little like smoke clearing, a little like a curtain rising, a little like the night was being pulled back into storage for the day. Jenna uncapped her blue pen and opened her cloth-covered journal.

"It's giving up," murmured Jenna.

"What's that?"

Maybe she didn't want company here. "The night is giving up. But not giving up like it's been beat. It's surrendering. No, that sounds like sheriffs and outlaws. It's—" No. Such a luscious word as the one on her tongue would make her turn red as a plum. And it was such a Lia word.

"It's what, girl?" asked Grandpa.

"Relinquishing." Oh, those were beautiful syllables.

Now a blister of blaze orange floated on the water. It was a burn, a sore that had to be borne before the glorious moment. Jenna's pen raced across the page. It was no wonder people used to think the sun went around the earth. Watching it rise before her, she wouldn't have blamed them if they thought the earth gave birth to the sun, maybe a new one every day.

She stopped writing abruptly. Maybe she would blame them. A funny feeling that she didn't quite understand came over her. It was as if—as if people who could think such a wrong thing must be people who had lost track of God.

"That's a pretty deep frown for a beautiful morning," Grandpa said.

"Grandpa, what does the sunrise mean?"

"Not sure I follow you."

"Why do people watch it?"

"'Cause nature puts on some spectacular shows." Grandpa shrugged. "And 'cause it makes a fellow's problems seem smaller. Don't sweat the small stuff 'cause the sun'll still come up tomorrow."

"Then the sunrise means hope," Jenna said.

"You got a good head on your shoulders for a kid your age."

"Did you ever think—" No. What was *she*

thinking, saying her thoughts instead of writing them in a book where they could be folded away?

"Think what, girl? You practice finishing those thoughts. Keep your mind working."

But Grandpa wasn't going to like this. "Did you ever think—the sunrise every morning was like God saying every morning, 'I'm still here'? Did you ever think—" Jenna gripped her pen. "Did you ever think that everything that happens in nature shows us one part of what God is like?"

Grandpa shook his head. "Can't say as I did. He may have started it all, but I don't believe God personally pushes the sun up every morning."

"Oh, I don't either," Jenna rushed. "I just think it's been obeying Him ever since He made it. I just mean God put all these different things around us to show us parts of Himself. We can't understand all of Him at once, but we can see pieces—" The words crumbled off her tongue. She had never spoken this way to anyone before except her best friend Kate, and she didn't understand what was pushing her now.

"One thing I do see." Grandpa turned his weathered face directly to her for the first time that morning. "You've got an idea that's lit a fire under you. Write it down, Jenna. Don't let it spill out your mouth. Write it down."

Jenna did, scrawling about the power of storms

and the largeness of space and the parts of atoms so tiny it took faith to believe in them.

The sun had risen now, riper than any peach Jenna had ever seen.

"Do me a favor, girl."

His gruff voice startled her back into the world. "Sure, Grandpa."

"Read me something you put down there. Just something. Any part."

"Read?" Jenna squeaked.

"Just once for your old grandpa."

"The sun rose like a ripe peach," Jenna began. "As it climbs—" Jenna squirmed.

"Just once." It was the gentlest voice she'd ever heard Grandpa use. "For your old grandpa."

"As it climbs, the bloody parts drain away, like—like a birth coating being shed, and the full-grown sun will shine pure yellow and stretch out its rays to the earth.

"Oh, that's terrible," Jenna howled, before Grandpa could.

"No sirree," said Grandpa. "Oh, I don't think you're supposed to start out talking about peaches and then switch to things getting born, but the getting born part's a good thought. With the number of babies you've had over at your place, a person figures you know a little what you're talkin' about."

"But the sun doesn't *get born*," Jenna said in a small voice.

"You can write it any way you want, girl."

But God, Jenna thought. Just those two words. She didn't know what came after "but God," but she wanted to say the words to Grandpa, to set them in front of him.

"You got the gift of words. I just wanted to hear them once. And they aren't half bad. Not half bad at all."

"But God," Jenna said.

Grandpa's smile was almost a laugh, but his closed lips kept it in. "But God what?"

"I don't know. Just—but God. I just have those two words right now."

As long as they stayed on the sand, Jenna thought, she could say any crazy things she had left to say. But time was short. It was full morning now. The breeze had started its day, small green waves dived onto the beach, and it was just as if they'd never seen the sunrise. Any minute they'd hear another voice, and that other voice would mean this time was over.

"Well, when you figure out the rest of the sentence, you write it down," Grandpa said. "And I promise you won't have to read it to your old grandpa."

"Stan!" A faraway voice reached out to them from the house. "Jenna? That you out there?

Breakfast."

"Grandma's got a spread waiting."

Jenna felt strangely heavy-hearted, but she was grateful to think of a way to end pleasantly. She smiled. "Better go on up and check it out."

Grandpa turned toward the house, but not before he let Jenna see the twinkle in his eyes.

Jenna got up from the sand and followed him, gazing at the huge honey-bronze and glass house built into a hill, climbing its steps behind Grandpa, hearing him puff.

She could call the cottage Hill House. No. Hill House might turn out to be part of the name, but the rest of the words were missing.

❦

"Hey, Mom, I'm gonna go shoot buckets with Greg." David got up from the breakfast table. He had already managed to meet a boy who lived down the road.

"Not now." Mom shook her head. "We need you for baby-sitting while we go into town this morning."

"What?" David's voice sailed higher than Jenna had heard it go in a whole year. "Coach says I have to shoot. He says good basketball players are made in the summer."

"Well, the morning of July eighteenth won't make or break your career," Dad said. "We're going into town with Grandma and Grandpa, and we need you."

"What about Lia?"

Jenna had wondered why Lia wasn't at the table.

"She doesn't feel well this morning," Mom said.

"What about Jenna?"

"She isn't twelve yet."

Hopes soaring, Jenna downed the last of her orange juice. She didn't usually like to hear she was too young for something, but if she didn't have to baby-sit, she could walk down toward Maralissa's.

"Everybody sits when they're eleven. Sherry can help her."

"And then you know what, David?" said Dad. "That age just keeps sliding downward. Pretty soon an *almost* eleven-year-old baby-sits. Then a *young* ten-year-old, and after a while you'll have eight-year-olds baby-sitting."

"I'm almost eight," Peter said importantly.

"Exactly my point." Looking at David, Dad cocked his head toward Peter. "In our family, a baby-sitter *left alone in charge* must be twelve."

Jenna got up and began gathering dishes. If she carried as much as she could to the dishwasher, she could probably escape notice and get out the door. Then she would have to make herself walk down the gravel road before the little kids all latched onto her. Her knees felt trembly.

"Jenna and Sherry can help by playing with the kids," Mom said.

Jenna stopped still on her way to the kitchen. "Aw, Mom!"

"You didn't have plans, did you?" Mom seemed surprised.

"She was going to go hide in the trees and day-dream about the beautiful hermitess." Cara sighed.

"Oh, I'll go!" Maria cried. "I brang dress-up clothes. We'll put on long skirts and journal to Mixed-Up Forest and build a house."

"Great. Then it's settled," Dad said.

Jenna sagged against the kitchen counter and groaned. It was great, all right. A whole morning spent refereeing little kids, but was she in charge? Oh no. She was subject to King David.

There were bumping sounds as people left the table. Jenna turned from the counter to see all her little Israelites running toward her.

"Batsister, will you please pin my cape on?" Ben held out to Jenna a faded and frayed green towel and a large diaper pin.

"Batsister?" David rolled off the couch, laughing and stamping his feet on the floor.

"Yes. I'm Batman," Ben explained, reasonable as a teacher. "Mom is Batmom, Dad is Batdad—"

"I get the picture," said David.

"And you are Batbrother."

"Cool."

"Put your head up so I don't pin your nose," Jenna told him.

"And Peter can be Robin, and Maria can be Catwoman, and—and Tyler can be Alfred!"

Ben caught the giggles and couldn't stop. Even Jenna laughed at the idea that plump, curly-haired, two-year-old Tyler would be Batman's old servant. "Batman" and "Robin" flew across the great room and made a great deal of noise turning an almost-empty bookshelf into the Batmobile.

Sherry approached Jenna quietly. "If we took Maria and Tyler with us, we could—you know, go look at Bluerose Cottage."

"No way," Jenna said automatically. Maralissa belonged to *her*.

"Why not?"

Jenna sighed. Sherry was probably right. Jenna could never be sure she'd get a chance to meet Maralissa without little kids tagging along. Even worse, if she refused, they might all just go to Bluerose Cottage without her. To top it off, Sherry was beginning to stand up for herself in quiet ways, and that made her more interesting to be around.

"Okay," Jenna agreed.

Maria issued dress-up dresses to Jenna, Sherry,

Cara, herself, and even Tyler. Jenna had a sudden idea. She whispered to Sherry, and they spent ten hurried, giggly minutes in the kitchen packing a paper sack.

"Climb-ing up the hill to Mixed-Up For-est," Maria singsonged as they set out. "We shouldn't have left our walk-ing sticks in the house."

Laughing, pretending to be shepherds, mountaineers, Moses, and Maralissa Rose, they reached the trees. Jenna was careful to steer them south until they almost broke through to the clearing where Bluerose Cottage stood.

"What's inna bag?" Tyler asked, poking at the sack.

"Gather round." Jenna sat down and spread her hands to indicate a circle. "In honor of our journey to Mixed-Up Forest, it is now time to have the mixed-up snack."

Sherry pulled a plastic bag out of the brown bag and passed half a sandwich to each person. Cara laughed, which surprised and pleased Jenna. "I get it. It's mixed up 'cause it's wieners in hamburger buns."

"In dere," said Tyler, patting the thermos bottle Sherry took from the bag.

"Pop," Sherry said. "Orange and grape mixed."

"Look!" Maria cried.

Jenna's head jerked up. Her eyes caught curves of airy white fabric, sheer as butterfly wings, behind the trunks and crisscrossed branches of the trees. She didn't fly away, but Maralissa Rose was too near not to have heard.

She stepped between the trees to face them, a wicker basket on her arm, her filmy dress flowing to her ankles. The basket held purple and yellow wildflowers. Maralissa's face was pale and not as beautiful up close as Jenna expected. The part in her hair was wide, but waves cascaded appealingly from a pearled barrette on top of her head.

Maria jumped to her feet. "Are you real?"

"Maria!" cried Jenna.

A smile tugging at her lips, Maralissa nodded.

"Are you Em-Emily Ricky-man? Jenna, what was that poet lady's name?"

"Maria!"

"We're just like you!" Maria shouted, holding her skirt out as if she were going to curtsey.

"Maria! We are not!" Jenna jumped up too. "We're not—I mean—" Oh, how was she supposed to tell Maralissa that in their long dresses they hadn't meant to copy her? Or mock her? Face burning, she thrust out the last half of sandwich. "Would you like a hotburger?"

Maralissa laughed—the short, warm sound of delight that a princess would use with children. Then she shook her head and disappeared through the trees.

"Well, she could have said something." Cara took a slurp of orange-grape pop.

"She wanted to be alone." Jenna stared after her, not blinking.

They passed the pop around until Maria's and Tyler's chins dribbled. Then they collected the uneaten parts of the sandwiches in the paper bag. But Jenna's attention had been drawn inside her own mind again. Maralissa had shied away because of the crowd, she felt. But if she, Jenna, were to call on her *alone*, maybe with a basket of flowers and an apology for disturbing her . . .

"I'ma go home." Jenna became aware of Tyler poking her arm.

"I'm sticky," Maria whined.

As their little group went down the hill, Jenna's heart rose instead, as if to lift her above the trees. Maralissa was a soul mate, a kindred spirit, and very soon now they would meet at Bluerose Cottage.

The Schellenburgs' house looked almost small from this direction, partly hidden by the hill, tucked securely into its side and camouflaged from the road by Mixed-Up Forest. Jenna imagined how forest animals would gather branches and grasses into cushiony roofs and then creep down into cozy burrows for sleep. Funny how this grand wooden house for humans seemed kind of the same.

The name came to her as they circled to the front. The steep, pointed roof and the sweeping panels of glass declared once again what a happy, sunny, airy, ship of a tree house this was.

The station wagon that her parents and grandparents had taken to town had come back. Grandma sat on the front seat with the door open, her feet on the blacktop.

"Grandma," Jenna called, forgetting the name was to be secret at first. "The name of your cottage is Happy Hill House."

"Kids." Suddenly Mom was with them, holding her arms out to take them into a circle hug.

Grandma looked tired, just sitting there in the car. Had they come home because she was ill?

"I'm afraid I have something sad to tell you." The wind blew spikes of hair across Mom's creased face. "I don't know if you realize it, but Grandpa has been a bit tired lately. This morning while we were shopping in town, he suddenly had a heart attack."

Mom paused to look at each child in the circle. She looked a little longer at Jenna and Sherry. "We called 911 right away and did CPR, but we weren't able to bring him back." Then Mom stooped to look at the younger children face to face. "I'm very sorry to say this, but Grandpa is dead."

❦ 5 ❦

Mixed Up

M OTHER, WOULD YOU LET US PRAY with you?"

All the Vander Giffins surrounded Grandma Schellenburg in the sprawling, plush-carpeted great room. The cool weather had given way to a real chill, and the wood stove radiated a steady heat that warmed their bodies, if not their souls.

"If you want to." Grandma stared vacantly. Her voice was thin and high. "For all the good it'll do. It's a little like locking the barn after the horse was stolen, isn't it?"

"Lord, thank You for bringing us here to help and comfort Mother during this time," Mom prayed. "We ask You to reach out to her with greater comfort, peace, and love than we can give."

"Lord," Dad continued, "we ask the same for the other families, for Bob's, Mike's, and Deb's families, and for John and Pam too, that You be with them as they prepare to travel at a difficult time. Bring them to us safely, Father."

None of the children spoke, and Jenna wondered if they, like she, were all too shocked. Grandpa just couldn't be dead. They'd sat on the beach together only hours ago. He'd spoken; afterwards he'd eaten. Such normal things. He'd said the sun would still come up tomorrow.

He didn't say which people it would shine on.

He didn't understand about God. About Jesus.

She hadn't finished her sentence that started, "But God." But God what? But God is there? But God loves you? The words had been missing. Grandpa said she had a gift for words, but when he turned to her for words, he'd got a silly passage about the sun getting born like a peach. He had turned to her for words, and she had not given him the right words.

But the Bible, the church, the Christians, the parents—all had words. Their words said that unless you go to Jesus for forgiveness of sins, you don't go to Heaven.

And Dad had prayed, and Mom had prayed, and the kids had prayed, and *she* had prayed, "Please help Grandma and Grandpa Schellenburg to know Jesus and go to Heaven." A dozen times.

Grandpa had just been here, in his flesh, with his gray head and the veins tunneling under the skin of his hands, his gruffly teasing voice, and his surprisingly young, strong arms. He'd been there behind his blue eyes.

How could it be that the last pleasure he'd ever had was watching a sunrise on a lake shore with Jenna? How could it be that this beautiful morning might be the last thing of beauty he'd ever see?

🍓

"Has Grandma got nineteen cots?" Melly Schellenburg buzzed into her cousin Jenna's ear.

"Well, no, they'd never fit."

Jenna and thirteen-year-old Melly were alternately helping and watching as the lofts filled with sleeping bags and air mattresses, knapsacks, and small zippered cases with "Going to Grandma's" printed on their tops.

"See, they brought their own stuff," Jenna explained. "And Uncle Mike and Aunt Nina and the T's are going to a motel."

"Tim, Tessa, Trevor, Travis, Tara," Melly recited, as they had when they were younger. Tara was a new addition to the list though, being only six months old. Maybe Melly felt she had to try out how five T's sounded.

Though Melly was thirteen, she wasn't Lia's kind of thirteen at all. She was plumpish and had frizzy light orange hair, but the real difference was that Melly was kind of simple. Jenna had thought

Melly might be calling herself Melanie by now, but she wasn't. Still, Jenna liked Melly's openness and good intentions, and she was a sister in the Lord as well as a cousin.

Maria and their six-year-old cousin, Kelli Cook, were giggling in a corner about Barbies. Kelli's mom, Linda Vander Giffin's look-alike sister Deb, was trying to sandwich dresses for Kelli and three-year-old Holli into the already overstuffed closet. Funeral dresses, Jenna knew.

Aunt Deb and Uncle Jim Cook had driven up all the way from Beloit, and they and everyone else had arrived tired, famished, and glazed with shock. Pizza was ordered. Card tables were set up. Milk was spilled. Cars drove in and out, taking a suit for Grandpa to the funeral home, bringing boxes of cereal for fourteen kids' breakfasts, running errands Jenna didn't understand but which involved a lot of decisions no one wanted to make. And now Jenna, Lia, Sherry, and Melly were to keep the peace among the girls, while David and Melly's brother Ryan were to ride herd on four little boys. The adults took turns comforting Grandma, crying themselves, slinking off to corners for sober conversations, or jumping into cars on some sudden urgent task. It was a circus, a zoo, and a party, and nothing that was said or done seemed completely appropriate.

"How could it happen?" Melly asked. "I mean, how can you just go to the store and—"

Jenna knew Melly had heard the story, because everyone had wanted to hear it over and over again. They wanted to work every detail out of Mom's and Dad's memories, as if knowing what had happened could help explain why. Of Grandma's memory, the adults, at least, were a little more careful.

"Didn't anyone tell you?" Aunt Deb gave up on the closet and turned to them. Her voice was tired but kind. "He collapsed in the grocery store."

"Collapsed? That's like—his legs fell out from under him?"

"Melly!" Jenna said. The trouble with Melly was that she had a lot of the same embarrassing thoughts Jenna had, but Melly actually said them. Jenna had always thought the word *collapsed* sounded like wood breaking and somebody falling down into the splits, but she kept such thoughts to herself.

"It's okay if you ask," said Aunt Deb. She pushed curly dark hair, shorter than Mom's and not braided, off her face. "Aunt Linda and Uncle Mark were the ones who were with him, but I know basically that's what happened. He fell. They called 911 right away, and Uncle Mark and a woman in the store did CPR, but they never got his pulse or breathing back."

"I just never saw an adult fall down," Melly said. "I mean it's hard to believe they really can. When somebody says an adult fell, like an old lady broke her hip or something, I sort of picture them sitting there, but I don't picture them *falling*. I just can't really believe—"

Jenna, who knew exactly what Melly meant, cried, "Melleee!"

Most of the loft, the girls' loft anyway, went silent while Melly was talking. Maria and Kelli sat wide-eyed. Cara watched with open interest, probably half hoping Melly would be reprimanded. Lia rested her forehead in her hand. Either she was feeling sick again, or she was praying to hold her tongue.

Aunt Deb flashed a small, amazed smile in Melly's direction; then it faded. "Well, they can fall."

Little Holli continued to work on her crooked somersaults. "Wats me, Mom. Wats me. Hey, wats me, Kewwi. Wats me." As Aunt Deb voiced her approval and left the room, Ben suddenly flew into the room and began giving her lessons.

"I just can't really believe it, can you, Jenna?" At least Melly had turned to Jenna and was keeping her voice down.

"Melly." Jenna grabbed her arm and tried to pull her out of the room. If she was going to chatter, maybe she could at least not do it in front of people.

"Where are you two going? You're supposed to help watch the kids," Lia challenged.

"Can you and Sherry? I think Melly . . ." She didn't want to add, "wants to talk."

"I'm sick."

"It's okay." Sherry shrugged.

"No, it isn't."

"Let 'em go." Cara snorted.

"I got a Barbie sports car.

"Wats me, Wia."

"Superman!"

". . . many Barbies do you got?"

"One, two, three—no. I have to think. One, two . . ."

"Wats me, Cawa."

"I think we're supposed to get their pajamas on!" Lia called to Jenna through her cupped hands. Then she raised her eyebrows.

So if Melly needed to talk, she would just have to wait, Jenna thought, as she helped Kelli paw through her Barbie overnight case in search of her Barbie nightgown. That was the trouble with needing to talk. Not only wasn't there time, but honest words like Melly's always made the truth hang there naked. People couldn't handle it.

Jenna needed silence. Silence was stronger. Before Grandma had fallen into silence, she had worn herself out telling the story over and over.

"He got the shopping cart for me like he always

does. I push it, you know, because if I don't, I always end up holding five pounds of potatoes and a watermelon, and he's clear over by the meat, but he pulled the carts apart for me at the door and got me one like he always does. And I had just picked up ten pounds of chicken drumsticks, and—" Grandma's voice had gotten higher and higher as tears threatened. "And he says to me, 'Dorothy,' he says, 'pick me up some of that pickled herring.' I was reaching for the jar, and I heard Linda call, 'Dad!' and I looked, and he was sort of sitting on the floor . . . Can you imagine? Those were his last words, 'Dorothy, pick me up some of that pickled herring.'"

Jenna's eyes flooded, and for a moment she couldn't sort out the top of Holli's shorty pajamas from the bottom. To think of Grandpa slumped on the grocery store floor . . .

Jenna worked her imagination as hard as she could. She thought Grandma must have told the story over and over because she could scarcely believe it herself. But what Jenna found hardest to bear was that the telling was a kind of begging. And when Melly kept saying how unbelievable it was, which was unnecessary because everyone knew that, it was like making Grandpa's death into gossip.

It was better to be silent. By keeping it inside herself, she didn't make it cheap, she didn't spoil it with the wrong words, and she didn't end up asking questions to which adults would say, "I don't know."

Because sometimes those words were just too scary. Seeing an adult fall was too scary. If they fell, who was left to take care of you? Was there really no one to depend on but Jesus?

Jenna was struck still by a deep, wordless thought: Everything she believed about God absolutely had to be true. If it wasn't true, then people's lives could blow up any time, and the only people who could help could blow up too.

"Dzenna, my dzammies!"

Jenna absently held out the pajama pants for Holli to step into and then made herself crawl to the nearby rumpled sleeping bags and smooth them out next to each other. She needed to touch something real, something real in this room that was less scary to think about than people.

But if everything she believed about God was absolutely true, how could she bear the thought that Grandpa was in—oh, it was such a reckless, violent-sounding word—*Hell?*

❧

"I'll watch the kids," Jenna said to Mom, as they filed out of the funeral home after the service. She figured she'd be asked anyway, and that way she could focus on people who were acting normal. She could also get her turn in to watch the kids while they were on pretty decent behavior. And maybe she wouldn't have to think about that pastor saying Stanley Schellenburg was more alive than any of them. How could he know? Grandma and Grandpa might be members of his church, but they hadn't attended in years.

"Well, I don't think the kids will need that much watching. We'll all be sitting together at the cemetery and the dinner." Mom's face was pale, the skin drawn vertical. "But if the little ones get squirmy—fine. Maybe we can get someone to watch with you."

"Not Melly."

Mom looked mildly surprised.

"A boy. From a different family. Ryan."

As it turned out the children didn't need much watching. Once Jenna had to chase two-year-old Travis, one of the five T's of Uncle Mike and Aunt Nina Schellenburg, across the cemetery. Before he could pick a geranium from a grave or play peek-a-boo over a headstone, Jenna caught him up and spun with him till he giggled like a music box. Then she set him down a distance from the funeral tent and led him by the hand back to the family.

And once, at the ham and potato salad meal in the church basement, she had to untangle Tessa

Schellenburg's dress from the hinges of the metal folding chair she was trying to squirm out of.

It was too bad the day couldn't be untangled as easily as Tessa's ruffled hem.

"Grandpa went to Hell, didn't he," Melly had said to her in the funeral home parking lot.

"Melly!"

"Well, didn't he? Who'm I supposed to—"

Jenna had stuck her fingers in her ears and run.

Now, sitting limply as the car hauled her back to Happy Hill House, Jenna wished she hadn't done it. Who *was* Melly supposed to say this to? Somebody who didn't believe the gospel and would say, "Of course he didn't, dear"? Or a grown-up who would shush her and—do just what Jenna had done?

Everything was mixed up, Jenna thought, as the tires crunched gravel. It was mixed up that she had named the cottage Happy Hill House on the day of Grandpa's death. It was mixed up that Tyler's second birthday had been yesterday, and he could unexpectedly eat hot dogs and cake with Mom's entire family. It was mixed up that a whole fleet of Schellenburg, Cook, and Vander Giffin cars was now crawling just like the funeral procession up the gravel road, past Bluerose Cottage, past Maralissa Rose.

"There's Malis-sara!" Maria cried.

Jenna would not look out the window. Just a

63

glance from a Vander Giffin mixed Maralissa up too. And as the gravel road passed Mixed-Up Forest and approached the blacktopped drive, Jenna covered her eyes.

❧ 6 ❧

Bluerose Cottage and the Baby-Sitting Blues

THE RELATIVES LEFT LITTLE BY little, like flocks of geese flying south. The Cooks headed back to Beloit the morning after the funeral. Uncle Jim couldn't take off much time from work. Uncle Mike and Aunt Nina and the T's stopped by the cottage in their van before they got on the road. Uncle Bob and Aunt Liz packed up Ryan, Melly, and Andy, and in shame Jenna waved Melly up the gravel path so hard and so far that she thought her arm might swing out of her shoulder. Last, Uncle John Schellenburg and Aunt Pam Schellenburg, Mom's brother and sister who were unmarried, pulled out in their rental cars to drive to some airport, from which they'd fly to their jobs in Chicago and Philadelphia.

And the Vander Giffins were left to start their vacation all over again.

"It might be quieter than we planned," Mom said.

"But Grandma needs us to stay with her for a while," Dad told them.

So they splashed in the cold lake, scooped and stirred the brown-sugar sand, grilled hamburgers and brats on the deck when it was warm, and allowed Grandma to gather them around the wood stove and cook for them when it wasn't. And one early evening Jenna found her chance to slip through the south end of Mixed-Up Forest and enter the grassy yard of Bluerose Cottage.

A banner of purple and yellow wildflowers, the kind Maralissa had carried in her basket, bloomed at her edge of the woods. The thick grass, long enough to mow, tugged at Jenna's shoes as she walked through it. A narrow garden planted with pansies and petunias—blues, whites, and pinks—ran along the side of the house, and in front Jenna found three small rose bushes. Each one wore two or three blooms. The bush on the left had red blossoms, the middle one had white, and the roses closest to the door were pink.

Jenna liked the red roses best, but it was the white bush she bent over to examine. She knew just how those creamy petals would feel: cool and buttery but not greasy, velvety but not fuzzy, like delicate skin but not papery. Her hand reached slowly forward, thumb and index fingers held like tweezers.

"Hello."

Jenna jumped backward and straightened up. Her guilty hand flew behind her. Before she could worry about how close she was to the cottage door and whether she should knock and what she'd say when Maralissa answered, here Maralissa stood. Her long dress was pale blue this time and textured with little puckers that Jenna could tell were supposed to be there. Her dark hair was pinned to her head.

"May I help you?"

"Uh—no! I just came down to see—I mean—I wasn't going to pick one of your roses, really I wasn't! It's just that the petals are so pretty all overlapped inside each other like that—"

Maralissa took something out of her pocket. Jenna was surprised that her kind of dress would have pockets. Drawing a thin blade from a pearled handle, Maralissa bent down and cut the very rose Jenna had been looking at. Her wrist was bony, and more bones fanned across the top of her hand like the tines of a rake. Straightening up, she handed the white rose, long-stemmed, to Jenna. "Be careful of the thorns."

"Oh, it's beautiful! Thank you." The petals felt against her cheek exactly the way she knew they would. The sweet perfume made her wish she could breathe in, in, in forever, without full lungs to stop her.

"I hope you understand—I won't have enough roses for your whole family."

"Oh, that's okay." Jenna's heart leaped. *This one is special for me.* "I'm sorry about the other day. I hope the little kids didn't bother you."

"Oh, you mean in the woods? That's no problem. The trees belong to your grandparents, you know. You're not trespassing."

"I mean, there *are* a lot of us, and lately us older ones have to take care of the little ones a lot."

"I'm sorry about your grandfather."

Jenna nodded.

"Well, I have to go in."

"I'll make sure the other kids don't bother you for roses." Jenna couldn't bear the thought that Maralissa might come to regret giving her the rose. "I'll keep it—"

No. There was exactly nowhere at Happy Hill House that she could hide a rose in a vase.

"I'll share it," Jenna said. "I'll put it on the dining room table where it can be everybody's."

Maralissa tipped her head a bit, and her eyes opened wider as if with new interest. Then she seemed to almost shake herself free of it. "I have to go." As lightly as if she weighed nothing, Maralissa slipped inside the stone entryway, and the door of Bluerose Cottage clicked shut behind her.

Wait, Jenna wanted to call. She hadn't had a chance to tell Maralissa about naming Happy Hill House. Not that the name seemed to fit anymore, with everyone kind of quiet about Grandpa's death. She hadn't even had a chance to tell Maralissa her own name.

She stood for a few minutes, just drinking in the sight of tiny Bluerose Cottage and its blue rose sign waving in the wind. Then, to show she wasn't a pest, just in case Maralissa was watching from a window, she turned and walked back toward Grandma and Grandpa's cottage. Grandma's cottage. And she thought that with all the things left unsaid, she would just have to see Maralissa again soon.

❦

"Jenna." Mom beckoned to her from the kitchen doorway the next morning as she was putting her cereal bowl and juice glass into the dishwasher. "I'd like you and Lia to watch the three youngest while we go into town."

"Mom!" Not only did this spoil Jenna's plans to see Maralissa, but she was horrified. This was Saturday morning, exactly one week after Grandpa . . . She shook her head to erase the thought. How could they want to go back to that store this morning? How could *Grandma* want to?

"I'll explain what's going on," Mom said. "Dad's driving home on some business just overnight. David and Peter are going with him. Grandma and I are taking Sherry and Cara into town for shopping and lunch." Mom held up her hand to forestall Jenna's protest. "We hope to do something like this with the rest of you too. Two at a time, maybe two who don't usually pair up with each other. Today it's Sherry and Cara."

"Two into nine doesn't come out even," said Jenna.

"We'll work something out." Mom waved this away. "This leaves you and Lia with Maria, Ben, and Tyler. You can have leftover spaghetti casserole for lunch. I'll leave microwave instructions for Lia."

"I know how to run the microwave. Hey wait, can I bake something?" A new plan was rapidly forming. "I haven't baked anything in a long time, and I'll bet Grandma will be surprised how good I am—I mean, not to brag or anything, but I am a good baker and—oh, please, Mom?"

Mom studied her. "You know how to work Grandma's stove?"

"I just need the temperature dial for the oven and the knob that changes from preheat to bake.

I'll only use the oven. If I have to melt butter or chocolate or anything, I'll use the microwave."

"You can find the pans and bowls and cups and everything?"

Jenna assured Mom that she'd learned where all these things were in the past week. And she would check that she had all of the ingredients before she started anything. She would not choose a recipe so hard that she'd end up neglecting the kids. In fact, they could help. All this seemed to satisfy Mom, so Jenna soon found herself alone with Lia, Maria, Ben, Tyler, and a kitchen just begging to be used.

"Remember when Cara wanted Baked Alaska for her birthday?" Jenna called to Lia. She had barely touched the cookbook when it fell open to a picture of a large cake heaped with ice cream and covered in golden meringue. Slices of the spectacular dessert lay just waiting for her to lift them onto china plates with a silver cake server. She smiled at the thought of the layer cake decorated with flowers that she'd served last month at Sherry's adoption dinner.

Lia was in the great room trying to persuade Tyler he needed to wear clothes. "I thought you weren't supposed to pick something hard."

"All this is, is a regular cake with ice cream on it and a meringue you only bake from three to five minutes. I can do this."

Lia came to the kitchen doorway and met her eyes. Jenna thought she would scoff or accuse her of not helping with the kids, but she did neither. "I'll just bet you can," Lia finally said.

Maria and Ben dragged chairs to the counter to help.

"We'll make a chocolate cake," Jenna said, stirring the shortening and sugar together. She loved all the different textures and tastes as she added ingredients one by one, so she almost never used a mix.

"Can I break an egg?" Maria asked.

"Can I have a lick?" said Ben.

"Can I go visit Mira-salla?" Maria chirped.

Jenna froze. She'd just given her egg a good crack on the edge of the bowl, and the contents slithered down both sides. She jerked her hand to make the egg spill inside and plucked out the shards of shell.

"I think she'd be good at playing dress up," Maria went on. "And she's big, so she could play tea party for real."

Jenna's Baked Alaska project was suddenly chaining her to the kitchen.

"I'll take the kids over there." Lia had finally stuffed Tyler into swimming trunks and a tank top. She appeared in the doorway, brushing her hair. "You can have the house to yourself while you work on the Baked Alaska."

Jenna found her voice. "No! Wait for me. I'll have the cake in the oven right away."

Lia looked amazed. "You can't leave."

"I'll set my watch to beep in thirty minutes." Jenna stuck her arm up to display her wrist.

Lia raised her eyebrows. "If that cake burns to an ash heap, it's your neck, Jenna."

Fifteen minutes later they finally assembled themselves and set off for Maralissa's. As they wove between the trees, Jenna felt a sense of doom. Maria had insisted on changing into a royal blue bridesmaid dress that Mom had worn at age sixteen for Uncle Bob's and Aunt Liz's wedding, and she was tripping every other step. Ben was wearing an especially tattered Superman cape. Tyler had screamed and cried at the thought of leaving without his toothbrushes, which he clamped in each fist the way other kids carried worn-out blankets. He had suddenly become too young to walk and now rode on Jenna's hip. She kept jutting her hip farther out and boosting Tyler up as she tried not to stumble on tree roots. Lia couldn't carry him, because she had dashed to the loft at the last minute and come back dragging her bedspread. "We may want to sit out under the pines," she had said grandly. Lia was hiding something under the spread too, but Jenna didn't know what it was.

"Hello," Lia began the instant Maralissa opened her door. "I'm Lia Vander Giffin." With a sweep of her hand toward each of her siblings, Lia gave their names. "It seems you've had to put up with us quite a lot lately, so we thought it would be polite to introduce ourselves."

The first flash of alarm on Maralissa's face was replaced by a more courteous expression, but for an awkward moment no one spoke.

"Are you Parunzel?" Maria piped up.

Jenna's eyes closed in embarrassment. "She means Rapunzel." As her eyes opened, a nervous giggle escaped her.

Then an odd thing happened. Maralissa, who had been looking blankly at Maria, straightened to her full height and felt her hair. She fingered the ends that hung from her silver barrette, as if she herself had to check how long her hair would hang if it were unpinned.

She let her hand drop to her side. Her smile was tight, but her eyes were dreamy. "I used to be."

Maria almost jumped out of her skin. "You used to be? Did you be-scape from the witch's tower? I bet you changed your name so she can't find you. Where's the handsome prince?"

Maralissa looked bewildered and very sorry she'd ever gotten into this.

"Did she cut your hair off, and did it start growing again?"

Maralissa's expression grew serious.

Maria finally ran out of steam. Her face wrinkled in confusion. "For real? Did you used to be Rapunzel for real?"

Eyes focused on Maria, Maralissa slowly shook her head.

"Oh. You're Maralissa for real then. Right?"

For once, Maria had said the name correctly. But Maralissa stared at Maria, astonished. Jenna instantly felt protective of her, and embarrassed and exasperated with Maria.

"Yes. Yes, I'm Maralissa." The woman added a nod after her words.

Tyler began struggling to get down. Lia made a "she's weird" face at Jenna.

"Rapunzel for pretend then," Maria said. "You must be a good pretender. Can we have a tea party with real tea? No, not tea. Just pretty cups that are real, and do you have grape juice to put in—"

"Maria!" Jenna cried.

"I really should—" Maralissa looked as if she wanted to add *go in,* but perhaps she thought it was too late.

"I'm Superman." Ben actually tugged at Maralissa's dress, which was the long white one today. "I fly and I fight crime and I'm a super hero."

"Ben," moaned Jenna.

"Not Ben. I am Clark Kent."

Tyler kicked Jenna again. Just as she gave in and let him slide down her leg, her watch beeped.

❧ 7 ❧

Fall-Apart Fairy Tales

"THIS IS A DISASTER," JENNA MUMBLED, zigzagging though the trees back to Happy Hill House. "What in the world did Maralissa think when I said, 'Oops, I've got a cake in the oven'?"

Jenna dashed to the oven, pulled the pan out, and poked the cake with a toothpick. It came out clean, so she knew the cake was done.

"I left her alone there with my weird brothers and sisters."

She took only a moment to twist the oven dial off and appreciate the warm chocolate smell.

"After this she'll lock her door whenever she sees any of us coming."

Jenna couldn't put ice cream on the hot cake, so she let the pan clatter onto the cooling rack. She spun around to dash out and ran full tilt into her brother Ben.

Ben fell over backward and hit the floor full-length. Pitching forward after him, Jenna jarred her wrists painfully as she tried to catch herself. Still she landed with most of her weight on Ben. He began to howl.

"Ben, why did you follow me back here?"

"Ow, oww, ooowww!" bellowed Ben.

Jenna got off him quickly. "Where do you hurt?"

"Oooowwww!" Ben screamed out a fresh lungful of air. Feet freed from under Jenna's body, he began to kick.

"Where does it hurt?" Jenna repeated. "Hey, settle down, huh. Your shoes in my stomach didn't feel so hot either."

"I'm Superman!" Ben roared. "I was supposed to get here first, and you beat me!"

"Is *that* why you're crying? You mean you're not hurt?" Jenna stood. "Ben Vander Giffin, get up off that floor."

"I am Clark Kent!"

"Well, I see Clark Kent's got his cape on. So come on, fly on back to Maralissa's." Jenna ran across the great room toward the sliding doors that led to the deck.

"Me first!" Ben shot to his feet.

Jenna moved aside to let him pass. It was the only way not to drive him completely crazy. If Superman was going to beat her to Bluerose Cottage, though, he'd have to hurry. She was going to fly there as fast as she could, cape or no cape.

Ben sailed through the sliding door, crossed the deck, and began to thunder down the wooden steps.

"Be caref—" Jenna got no further.

It almost seemed as if her very warning tripped him. The heel of his shoe caught on the edge of a step and flung him forward. He dived and began to roll sideways. Screaming, Jenna chased him to the bottom where he landed with a soft plop and lay still.

"Ben!" Jenna stumbled to his side. "Oh, Jesus, please make him be all right."

Ben was already whimpering and stirring. He sat up.

"Are you okay?"

Ben reached out his arms and clutched Jenna around the neck, sobbing. He sounded more frightened than hurt. Holding him in a limp bundle on her lap, Jenna sank against the bottom step and let her heart slow down to normal. If he hadn't cracked his head open like a coconut, at the very least all his bones must be jangled out of joint.

But he hadn't landed on any boulders or on the driveway several feet away. He had just landed in the sparse grass and dirt, which coated his body with a fine dust that turned to tracks of mud on his teary, sweaty face. His crying quieted.

"You okay?"

Ben nodded and scrubbed his eyes.

"You need a bath."

"Later. I'm going to Maralissa's."

"You sure you're okay?"

"I am Superman." With that he took off toward Mixed-Up Forest.

Jenna followed, trotting faster and faster as she remembered how quickly she wanted to get back. When she broke through the trees into Maralissa's yard, she stopped still.

She heard Lia's flute solo first, a haunting, yearning melody Mom said came from a *Romeo and Juliet* movie. It was the flute case she'd hidden under the bedspread. Lia and Maralissa were sitting on the spread under the pines, while the little kids, including Ben, gamboled and cavorted around them. How had—oh, didn't it just figure? Lia had lured Maralissa out of her house like the Pied Piper, and Jenna hadn't even had a chance to see how she did it. She approached them at a walk.

"Romeo and Juliet is almost a fairy tale," Lia said, the last plaintive notes of her song dying out. "They're beautiful and rich and in love, and there's evil and a magic potion—but the ending is sad. They die."

Maralissa was staring at Lia as if she'd never heard such an unbelievable plot.

"You know the story, don't you?" Lia said this carefully, as if she were speaking to Melly.

"Oh, of course." Maralissa seemed to shake herself out of a trance. "Everybody knows Romeo and Juliet." Her voice wavered to a halt, and her gaze fell to the bedspread, where it stuck.

"Jenna," Lia said cheerily, "I think we should round up these kids and leave Maralissa in peace." There was an edge of desperation in her voice. She began packing up her flute in an unnecessary hurry.

"Everybody knows Romeo and Juliet?" Maria began whirling in circles around Maralissa. "They are love birds, right?"

"You might have to carry Tyler," Lia told Jenna pointedly. Jenna could tell she meant, *Pick him up and let's get out of here*.

"I told Maralissa you made Baked Alaska." Maria still danced, the ruffled hem of her royal blue gown tearing a little more each time she stepped on it.

Thanks a lot, Jenna thought. *There goes my surprise—*

"Did you really, Jenna?"

Jenna turned quickly to Maralissa, still sitting on the bedspread. Maralissa was looking back at her with actual interest.

"I'm not even sure what it is," Maralissa added with a half-embarrassed laugh. She rose slowly from the bedspread, and Lia lost no time snatching it up. "I just know it's a fancy dessert."

"Cake with ice cream and meringue. It's really nothing. I mean, it is, it's great, but it's not that hard—" Jenna sighed. This had seemed like a promising subject, but she ran out of words so quickly. She held Maralissa's gaze until she had to look away.

"Denna! Losted toos-buss!" Tyler cried.

"You can have mine," Lia said. "Just let's get home before we get in trouble."

"What trouble?" Jenna asked as Tyler began to cry.

"Honestly, Jenna, you're as bad as Maria. 'Bye, Maralissa. It was nice meeting you and thanks for the visit."

Jenna smiled and murmured a goodbye over her shoulder before hoisting the screaming Tyler and trailing after her family. Lia waited for her in Mixed-Up Forest and pounced on her as soon as she reached the trees.

"Jenna, she is *weird*. What kind of person says she used to be Rapunzel? She hardly seemed to know her own name, and she gawked at me like an alien when I talked about Romeo and Juliet. Not only is she weird, she's boring. I'm never going there again."

"Maybe she's Juliet," Maria said. "She got all sad when you told the story because she can't find her true love Oreo."

"Romeo!" thundered Lia.

For once barely noticing Tyler's roaring in her ear, Jenna wondered if Lia was right. Of course Maralissa wasn't Juliet, but maybe the Rapunzel and Juliet stories reminded her of tragic memories. Maybe she was a sad, lonely woman cast away from all she held dear. If not, then why *did* she react so strangely to the stories, and why *did* she seem for a moment to forget her own name?

Lord, Jenna prayed as she had once before, *who is my neighbor?*

8

Vegetables and Baked Alaska

AFTER SUPPER JENNA CAREFULLY centered a slice of Baked Alaska on the prettiest dessert plate she could find and slid it into a loose plastic bag. Holding it in both hands, she picked her way carefully through Mixed-Up Forest toward Bluerose Cottage, her gaze jumping between the plate and her feet all the way.

Maralissa was outside with her back to Jenna, watering her pansies and petunias with a sprinkling can. In addition to the long dress, she was wearing a straw hat with a blue ribbon and clusters of something circling its crown. From the back, at least, no hair showed.

"Maralissa?" Jenna was afraid of startling her. She tried to make her voice move into the air gently.

"Hello, Jenna."

It was Jenna's turn to be startled. She hadn't been sure Maralissa would remember which one she was. She thrust the plate forward and thought suddenly of the hotburgers. "It's Baked Alaska. I really did make it."

"I know." Maralissa smiled and set down the watering can. "When Maria spilled the news, I could tell I was getting the truth."

"Maria can't *ever* keep her mouth shut. I'm sorry about all that noise before."

"Don't apologize for your family. It was a very interesting visit."

Jenna quickly studied Maralissa's face, wondering what she meant. She had looked stupefied most of the time, not interested. Was she making a joke? But Maralissa's expression was faraway, thoughtful.

The straw hat hid most of Maralissa's hair, even in front. She wasn't wearing a stroke of makeup. Her cheeks were thin, her skin pale with a spattering of freckles across the nose. Her brows were untweezed and wide as a finger. Jenna wondered with sudden hope whether she and Maralissa looked a bit alike. She almost reached up to feel her own heavy brows. Instead, Maralissa reached out to accept the plate. Jenna's heart soared.

Maralissa got a fork and led Jenna to sit on the concrete stoop tucked just inside the stone arch that guarded her front door. "I should get some lawn chairs."

"Oh, no—" Jenna broke off in confusion. Usually she would keep her real feelings to herself, and here she was blurting them out. "I like sitting inside here. I mean, under the arch." Her voice sounded squeaky. "It's cozy."

She sneaked a look at Maralissa, who was balancing the dessert plate on her muslin-covered knees. Jenna dared to let her gaze follow the first forkful of Baked Alaska to Maralissa's mouth. She was glad Maralissa hadn't felt she should put it in the freezer to eat later. Maybe she understood what it would mean to Jenna to see her enjoying it.

"Delicious," Maralissa pronounced.

Jenna hadn't noticed she'd been holding her back straight and tense, but now she sagged in relief.

"Was it hard to make?"

"Only when I ran the mixer."

"Meringue is tricky."

"No, I don't mean that," Jenna said. "I mean I don't like the noise of the mixer." She was aware of Maralissa studying her. "Oh, sometimes I do because you can be alone in a loud noise if it's really loud. And sometimes it's exciting because the noise is wild, but it all stays in the bowl. It's like safe danger. But today it was like—" She didn't want to finish, but it seemed impolite not to. "Sirens."

And sirens had made her think of Grandpa. Then, listening to the motor labor as the meringue puffed up to a taffy cloud all on one side of the bowl, she had wondered if Grandpa was in some sort of place where screaming, whirring, grinding, and scraping noises never stopped.

"I know what you mean," said Maralissa quietly. "That's why I don't water flowers with a hose."

Jenna forgot her mood. "Hoses aren't noisy!"

Maralissa laughed self-consciously. "No, but I don't like stretching the whole thing from the faucet to the garden and then winding it up afterward. I don't like it when the water rushes out faster than I want it to, and I have to dash back to the faucet. Sprinkling cans are peaceful. I guess I just like simple machines." She paused. "But the can does get heavy."

"Did you know that our house is called Happy Hill House?" Her eyes met Maralissa's again.

"Do you mean your grandparents' cottage or your house at home?"

"Oh, I mean here."

"Did *you* name Happy Hill House?" Maralissa looked very interested to hear the answer.

"Yes. My Grandma let me. It really is the house's name!"

Maralissa nodded.

"But maybe she forgot." Jenna looked straight ahead again, gazing across the gravel road into a jungle of green leaves. "I named it the day Grandpa died. Maybe she'll never think it's a happy house again."

"Oh, she will." Maralissa cut a straight line with her fork through the Baked Alaska left on her plate. "She will."

"Maybe we won't."

Maralissa turned her whole body and looked hard at Jenna then. "You miss him a lot, don't you?"

Jenna nodded because she thought she should, but she hadn't been thinking about missing him. Her heart began to pound. She'd been thinking about the silent, hollow shock of his sudden death, but even more she'd been thinking about where Grandpa might be now. She'd been thinking that when Grandpa asked her for words, she should have talked to him about Jesus and God, and she'd come far too close to saying this to Maralissa.

"It'll get easier."

Jenna nodded again.

"Well, I should be going in. I'm going to save the rest of your Baked Alaska till tomorrow." One neat half of the dessert still lay on the plate. She got up, and her dress swung softly around her ankles.

"Oh." Jenna jumped up too, not wanting the visit to end. "I really like your roses!" *That's stupid*, Jenna thought with a grimace. *She knows that*. "Oh, and the flowers on the side of the house. I can tell you work hard watering them." She almost groaned. What did people who liked to chatter all the time find to talk about?

Maralissa, wrapping her leftover Baked Alaska in the plastic, turned to her with the slight, amused smile that was becoming familiar. She laughed. For a moment Jenna felt terrible, but it wasn't a making-fun laugh. It was a delighted, twinkly-eyed, I-give-up kind of laugh, and in an instant Maralissa had reached out and grabbed her hand.

"So tell me, Jenna Vander Giffin," Maralissa said, striding with her toward the back yard, "do you like vegetables as much as you like flowers?"

She must have wrinkled her face because Maralissa laughed again, and this laugh was almost a hoot.

"Well, then, maybe my vegetable hat will help you appreciate them."

Maralissa's straw hat suddenly landed on Jenna's head. She snatched it off and looked at it. The clusters she'd seen earlier were bunches of vegetables—tiny carrots, tomatoes, potatoes, fans of string beans and pea pods, even shiny purple eggplants. "Cool."

Proudly, she put the hat back on.

"My garden doesn't have that much variety." Maralissa had put her dessert in the house, and now she led Jenna to a small plot not far from a hedge of thick bushes and a maple tree. "I just have zucchini, cucumbers, tomatoes, and beans."

"No corn?" Jenna asked. The garden was planted in neat rows, but Jenna couldn't tell one bunch of green leaves from another. She could almost like vegetable gardens that had tall, tasseled stalks and sweet yellow ears hidden beneath all the papery leaves.

"Corn is your favorite? Mine, too." Maralissa said this as if it were no surprise to her. "The other vegetables taste delicious home grown, and they're good for you, but corn is the fun vegetable. It's sweet, and it's for parties."

"And it's okay to get messy when you eat it. Why don't you have any?"

"I guess I thought it would be ready too late—" Maralissa clipped off the end of the sentence very fast.

"Too late for what?"

"I mean, I guess I thought it would be too much for me to eat. And it would be too late to share it because by the end of August, when it's ready, most of the neighbors will leave."

"Oh."

"I wish I'd put some in." Maralissa stared wistfully at the garden for a moment and then turned toward Bluerose Cottage. "Now I really do have to go in," she said as they walked past the row of flowers to the front yard. "Thanks for the visit and the great dessert, Jenna. By the way, my last name is Rose. Maralissa Rose."

"I know," Jenna told her.

Before closing her door, Maralissa flashed the amused smile again. "I'm not surprised."

❦

That evening before the gray, buff, and rose-colored streaks faded completely from the sky, Jenna carried her Bible up the hill to the edge of Mixed-Up Forest.

She thanked the Lord that Maralissa was her friend. Then she found her place in Luke and read that people should tell others they belong to Jesus. If they did this, Jesus would announce all over Heaven that they were His people. But if they rejected Him, Jesus would announce that *He* rejected *them*.

Dear Jesus, did that happen to Grandpa?

Jenna quickly turned a few pages, but there seemed to be no escape. "Sir, will just a few people be saved?" someone was asking. She skimmed

Jesus' answer. Was He going to tell how many people were going to Heaven?

No, He didn't. But He said lots of people would come to the Kingdom from all over, and others would have to sit outside and cry.

Oh, Lord, is Grandpa doing that?

She had a sudden, awful idea that lots of people were doing that. Then she thought of Maralissa, and her heart began to pound. She knew the temperature was dropping, and a fresh breeze was whispering on the hill, but her blood beat as if she were a furnace.

Tell Maralissa about You? Oh, Lord, I can't. I'm too scared.

Jenna shut the Bible, shivering. The black curtain over the sky had closed below the trees now, so she had an excuse to go in.

She had always been told that the Bible was good to read, and she'd thought that meant it would be comforting and gentle, with nothing worse than a list of rules about how people should act.

She wasn't sure she'd ever been told that sometimes it asked people to do something that was just plain scary.

❦ 9 ❦

The Address-Book Adventure

"SUNDAY, TODAY IS SUNDAY. GET IT?" Cara was standing on her head in the great room, bathed in the sunlight that poured through the floor-to-ceiling glass. Her shirt fell away from her waist, and her shadow seemed to grow from her head across the carpet, tall as a totem pole.

"Uh, Mom," Mom said to her own mother, "the kids and I are going to have . . . devotions. Would you like to come?"

Grandma sat at the dining table, sipping a mug of coffee. She still wore her bathrobe and the slippers that looked like dust mops. "No." She shook her head. Deep wrinkles branched out from her eyes and mouth.

The phone rang. Tyler, Ben, Maria, and Lia ran to get it.

"Jenna!" Maria yelled.

Jenna got up from her breakfast, surprised. Who would call? It could only be . . . Her heart began to pound.

"It's the beautiful princess, Missa-ralla. *What's* her name again?"

"Maria."

"Can I go, too? I want to play in her cottage. I want to see when the magic fairies come to bring her to the castle."

"What?"

"To get her crown. So she can really be the princess and then grow up to be the queen. Or is she grown up already? She doesn't seem grown up." Before Jenna could wrestle the phone from Maria's grip, Maria clamped it to her ear and cried, "Are you a girl or a woman?"

"Maria!" Jenna pried Maria's fingers from the receiver. "Hello?"

"Jenna? It's Maralissa. I found something special here at Bluerose Cottage that I think you'd like to see. Would you like to come over—when you're dressed and you've had breakfast and everything?"

Would she! "Oh, I'm dressed! And I'm just getting done with breakfast now."

Then she saw Mom across the great room with her Bible and some beach towels tucked in the crook of her arm. Mom was trying to persuade Cara to come down from her third or fourth headstand. The other kids looked more or less ready to follow her out onto the sun-drenched deck. As Cara thumped over in a full-length somersault and picked herself up, Mom turned and met Jenna's eyes. "Hurry up," she mouthed.

"Great," Maralissa was saying. "And, Jenna, is there anyone else—"

"Maralissa?"

"Yes?"

Jenna's heart pounded. It was hard enough to explain that she couldn't come right away, and now the family was listening avidly to her end of the conversation.

"I can't come right now. I mean, I can *come*, but first I have to—uh, well, I've got something to do for a little while before."

"Oh, that's fine, Jenna. Come down when you can. The weather's beautiful, so it looks like we'll have all day."

So the special something is outside.

"Jenna? I meant to ask . . . I'm not sure how to put this. Is there someone else in your family like you? I mean a sister you're especially close to or who's a lot like you?"

Not Maria.

"I'm not sure, but it might be best if she's not too little."

Sherry?

"It would be best if you brought one girl along. But just one."

"Okay." Jenna's curiosity was completely aroused. Across the great room, the rest of the kids were getting antsy, and Mom's eyebrows were rising higher and higher. Probably the only reason Mom didn't end the phone call right then was that Maralissa was an adult.

"See you later then, Jenna."

"See you."

Jenna followed her family through the sliding glass doors, clumped across the deck and down the wooden steps with all the other feet, and cut across the sparkly black driveway. Jenna couldn't get her mind off Maralissa's secret. What special thing had she found, and why did they need good weather? Why was it best to bring another girl who was something like herself?

Mom led them across the spiky grass to the warm bed of sand on the shore. The sand didn't scorch their feet this early in the day; it just lay before them like nature's electric blanket.

Like God's electric blanket.

Jenna stiffened. Her hands clenched the sand they'd begun to burrow in so casually, and she felt the grains push under her fingernails. What was God like if He gave His people a warm comfort that was yards wide and miles long, that they could dig into and roll over and over on and bury themselves in?

And what if God gave it to them on the very morning they couldn't even admit straight out to a friend that they were having family devotions?

She sat down on one of the beach towels Mom had spread on the sand, bumping arms with Lia, who finished pulling her hair back into an elastic band and began spreading sunscreen on her legs. Mom opened her Bible, and Jenna listened long enough to hear that at least she wasn't reading from Luke.

❦

"She asked me to bring you," Jenna explained to Sherry as they cut through Mixed-Up Forest. Jenna sighed with relief as Happy Hill House disappeared from view behind the thick trees. She'd had to promise Maria a candy bar, a dollar, and her own visit to Maralissa's the very next day in exchange for not following them now.

"Oh," said Sherry.

"I don't mean I didn't want you to come. I mean she invited you special."

Sherry's chin-length blonde hair seemed to swing closer around her face, as if preparing to hide it. "I didn't know she would know my name."

"She asked me," Jenna chose her words carefully, "to pick the oldest sister I had who was most like me."

"Ohh."

A world of pleasure shone forth from Sherry in that one syllable. Jenna basked in the glow. Sherry's adoption into the family had become final only a month before, and if Jenna had at times wondered how to find a place in their huge household, Sherry must have wondered even more. Jenna knew how much the word *sister* meant to her.

Maralissa answered Jenna's knock immediately. Jenna's eyes flew open, and she instinctively stepped back to look at Maralissa full length. She was wearing shorts!

Maralissa laughed. "Yes, I really have got legs under those long skirts. But today we need work clothes. I'm glad to see you girls are wearing your shorts and joggers."

"What is it?" Jenna could barely contain herself long enough to introduce Sherry to Maralissa. "What's going on?"

Maralissa sat down on the stoop under the stone arch. Jenna immediately joined her. Sherry didn't sit on Maralissa's other side, but nestled close to Jenna.

"Well, Bluerose Cottage isn't as new as Happy Hill House," Maralissa began. "I guess it was built about twenty-five years ago. I found this in the window seat in the loft."

She has a loft? Jenna thought, but she pushed this lovely idea aside until later. On her lap Maralissa placed a shiny white book decorated with large purple flowers. It had a spiral binding and little tabs with letters of the alphabet sticking out from the pages. A word curled across the cover in gold script: *Addresses*.

"Look at the first page," said Maralissa.

Jenna read:

> *Hi, I'm Peggy Carver. I'm ten years*
> *old, and today is August 11, 1978.*
> *Welcome to the Address Book*
> *Adventure.*

"Who is Peggy Carver? Do you know her?" asked Jenna.

"No. I think she belonged to the family who lived in the cottage before me," replied Maralissa.

"1978!" Even when excited, Sherry usually spoke softly. "We weren't even born yet."

Jenna continued reading:

> *Take with you: At least one friend.*
> *Two is better. The address book. A*
> *pen. A tape measure. A garden trowel.*
> *Two is better. Go!*

Jenna felt she should leap up and start running.

"Is there a time clock?" Sherry asked.

Jenna noticed a paper bag that must have been next to Maralissa the whole time. "Is that the—" She checked the address book. "The tape measure and the pen and the garden trowel?"

"Two is better." Maralissa nodded and patted the bag. "You'd better read one more instruction."

> *Next to us is the woods. There's a big field on the other side of the woods with big stones in it. My brother calls it Boulder Field, and he thinks this is really funny because it rhymes with Soldier Field, which I guess is in Chicago, and they play football there or something, but who cares.*

Maralissa laughed.

Jenna cried, "She means our yard!" She read on:

> *If there was a house in the woods, its number would be two more than ours is. If there was a house in the field, what would its number be?*

"Oh this is hard," said Sherry.

"Is it all going to be arithmetic?" Jenna fretted.

Then they looked at each other and laughed with relief. "We already know because there *is* a house! Grandma's number is fourteen," Jenna said.

"And Bluerose Cottage is number ten, and a house in the woods would be twelve," Maralissa added. "So I think fourteen is the number Peggy had in mind."

Jenna turned back curiously to the address book.

> *Add the digits of your answer. Go that many blocks north on Lake Road to the Grand Hansen Oak. It'll be there. My Aunt Bess Hansen said anybody who tried to cut that tree down would have to tie her up first.*

They all laughed.

> *Hole on east side of tree.*

"Here's where the hiking part comes in," said Maralissa. She grabbed the paper bag, and they hurried to the gravel road, which as Jenna expected was Lake Road. They crossed it in order to walk on the left.

"How do we know how far five blocks is?" Jenna asked. "There aren't street corners we can count, are there?"

"I think the house numbers will get into the twenties and thirties and so on," said Maralissa. "We should start watching when we get to the fifties. Any other ideas how we might know where it is?"

Jenna wasn't sure she was in the mood for thinking. The outdoors here was made up of stirrings: whispering leaves, sudden sharp rustlings of hidden animals, gravel sounding underfoot like fingers raking through marbles. Doilies of sunlight displayed sparkly stones and sprigs of wildflowers.

"That's *what* kind of book you have there?" teased Maralissa.

"Look her up!" Sherry hollered. "Look up the lady who said they'd have to tie her up."

"Aunt Bess Hansen." Jenna paged to the *H*s.

Ed and Bess Hansen
52 North Lake Road

The Grand Hansen Oak was obvious when they saw it. It stood alone at the edge of the road as if everything else had to grow at a respectful distance. If anyone ever did cut it down, its trunk would be as wide as a table. Its branches reached up so high into the sun that Jenna was blinded trying to see the tops of them.

The three crossed the road to check the east side of the tree.

"There's a hole," Sherry said.

Maralissa knelt, peered into the hole, and then stuck her left arm in gingerly and poked around. Satisfaction suddenly gleamed on her face. She pulled out a dirty jar filled with stones and a slip of paper. The note said:

Boulder Woods West. Siamese Twin Tree.

"Boulder Woods must be Mixed-Up Forest," Jenna said. "And the west side must be the part by the road. That's where the sun sets."

Her favorite part of the woods must be south, she reflected. There was no Siamese Twin Tree in that stand of trees between Happy Hill House and Maralissa's. Anyway, Peggy Carver probably would have called that the *north* part. Those trees were south of Happy Hill House, but they were *north* of Bluerose Cottage!

Jenna sank down. She felt dizzy, as if thoughts about directions were too powerful a current for the simple wires in her head. Maybe the wires had shorted out, and now every time she heard *north* or *east* or *south* or *west,* her brain would throw sparks and give her an eye-clenching, temple-pounding headache. "Poor Jenna," people would say, shaking their heads. "She's having one of her spells."

"So now we go all the way back?" asked Sherry.

"We'd have to anyway," Maralissa said.

Jenna suddenly noticed that Maralissa's voice seemed tired, and she hadn't gotten up since finding the jar in the tree.

"I've been glad for the rest," she added. Then she smiled. "But I can't wait to get to the end of this. Let's find the Siamese Twin Tree."

Peggy Carver wasn't making it too hard on them. The Siamese Twin Tree stood in the west part of Mixed-Up Forest, as obvious as the Grand Hansen Oak. Several feet from the ground its trunk suddenly split in opposite directions, giving the appearance of a wishbone. Nearly identical sets of branches and leaves curved like fans on either side.

Sherry found the hole and pulled out an even dirtier jar than the first, but none of them could budge the lid.

"We'll have to break it," Jenna said, not liking the idea.

"Here." Maralissa took the tape measure, pen, and trowels out of the paper bag and put the jar in it. She tapped on the outside of the closed bag with a trowel until they heard the tinkle of broken glass. With two fingers she withdrew the note.

> *C book twelve.*

Jenna muttered, "C book twelve?"

"See book!" Sherry exclaimed. "Look under *C*."

On the *C* page Jenna found more instructions.

> *Center of lilac bushes back of Carver land. Measure out number of feet given in note. Do this in the same direction as side of Twin Tree where you found hole.*

Jenna winced in case a Direction Headache should hit.

Dig same number of inches down.

"Well, that's in back of Bluerose Cottage," Maralissa said.

"What lilac bushes?" Jenna asked as they trotted through the trees with their trowels and tape measure and pen and rumpled bag of broken glass. "I didn't see any lilacs." She closed her mouth quickly, afraid she might be bothering Maralissa, who wasn't exactly trotting. She still seemed tired. *But after all*, Jenna thought, *my voice sounds huffy and puffy too.*

"I wouldn't have missed lilacs," Jenna added softly.

"I'll bet you wouldn't have."

Was that teasing in Maralissa's voice, Jenna wondered, treating her like a little girl? Or was it more like—*fondness?*

"Lilacs bloom in May," puffed Maralissa. "I missed them too."

"Maybe next year we can come in May!" Jenna crowed, excitement making her forget about keeping her voice down.

Maralissa didn't reply as they rounded the corner of Bluerose Cottage to the back yard. At once Jenna recognized the lilacs as the tall, thick bushes by the vegetable garden, near the pretty maple tree.

"Let's find the center," said Maralissa.

"We have to measure out twelve feet," Sherry put in. "That's the number in the note."

"Which way?" asked Maralissa. "I would guess toward the shore, but . . . Jenna, you've got the book."

> . . . *same direction as side of Twin*
> *Tree where you found hole.*

Jenna read through almost clenched teeth. She exchanged glances with Sherry, and Sherry shrugged.

"The hole was away from the road," Jenna said almost nervously. "That's going downhill toward the lake—*eeeeast!*" she yelped.

"It is on the beach then," said Maralissa. Jenna liked the satisfied tone in her voice, as if she wanted to solve this mystery as much as the girls did.

"East." Jenna nodded and smiled. The word didn't hurt a bit.

"Twelve feet east from the center of the bushes," Maralissa summed up. "Twelve inches down."

With their tape measure they worked their way out to a spot on the sand and began to dig with the two trowels. Sand flew in the air, stinging their eyes and clinging to their sweaty skin.

"Maybe over here a little."

"Here, you rest and I'll dig now."

"I wonder if anybody's looking at us."

Maralissa, kneeling in the sand, sank back on her heels. A large comma of hair escaped its silver clip and slid lazily down her left cheek.

Jenna, too, felt ready to quit. It was disappointing to find nothing now. All the other steps of Peggy Carver's treasure hunt had worked so well after so many years. But maybe whatever she'd buried had been dug up long ago or had been ruined or decayed in the ground or had sunk much lower than twelve inches. She had hardly finished the thought when her trowel hit something so solid that pain jolted her wrist. "Over here!"

Only a few swipes of the trowels uncovered the buried object. In unison they gasped.

"It's a real treasure chest!" Sherry cried.

❧ 10 ❧

Laundry Lessons

MARIA WILL HATE US, JENNA thought as they fought to free the small chest from the sand and pry it open with the tools. *Maria will be so mad that she missed this.*

"Ooof!" Maralissa cried as the lid gave way. "Careful, I cut my hand a little."

"You look in the jar, Jenna," said Sherry.

Jenna picked up the baby food jar that had been tucked into the treasure chest jewelry box. Fortunately the cap came off with only a little grunting. Inside were a note with blurred ink and three rings whose stones were red, blue, and green.

Jenna read from the note:

> *Congratulations! You've completed the Address Book Adventure. I bought the rings at KMart in Appleton. Mine's yellow. Please wear*

yours and think of me and each other.
We are all friends now!
    Keep my address book. Add your
names and your friends' names, even
if they move. If you check the Ks,
you'll see my best friend Mandy
Kaiser moved four times! But I
haven't lost her yet.

Jenna put the book down. All three stayed sitting on their legs in the sand, saying nothing. Jenna laid the three rings on her palm and stretched out her arm. Maralissa and Sherry reached together, and it happened very naturally that the green ring went to Sherry and the blue to Maralissa, leaving the rich wine-colored ring for Jenna. They solemnly slipped the rings on their fingers.

Jenna dared to break the silence. "Wouldn't it be fun to meet Peggy Carver?"

"We could look for her," Sherry said. "We've got her address book for clues."

"I wonder," said Maralissa softly, "why she left her address book in the window seat. I wonder why she would give it up just to use it for a treasure hunt for people she'd never know."

After a short silence Sherry answered, "Maybe she got a new one."

Maralissa turned to her and smiled gently. "She probably did."

"Because some of the pages are almost full with names and scribbled-out addresses."

"That must be it."

"Let's put in our addresses." Sherry picked up the book and pen and paged to the *V* section. "Wait. Do we put in our address here or the one at home?"

Jenna took only a moment to think. "Peggy Carver would say to put in both."

Maralissa smiled broadly at Jenna and tipped her head in that slight way as if she'd just been enchanted.

Jenna watched Sherry smile too—a little secret, satisfied smile. She wrote her name, Sherry Vander Giffin, not once but twice, followed by her address on Nicolet Street at home and her address at her grandmother's cottage on Lake Road.

Jenna added hers after Sherry's, but Maralissa wrote down just one address.

"This is my only home now," Maralissa said.

Jenna knew exactly what Maralissa meant. She meant she'd be using Bluerose Cottage as a year-round home rather than only a summer place.

Then why had such a funny thought come into her mind at Maralissa's words? It wasn't the kind of thought Maria would have. Maria would ask if Maralissa had been banished from the palace.

Jenna's funny thought was that what Maralissa had said wasn't really a Christian thing to say.

Adults and pastors were always saying that Heaven was their real home, and they were just here on earth for a stay. They wouldn't say a little cottage on earth was their only home.

But Maralissa didn't mean that kind of stuff, Jenna argued with herself. She sighed. Now she was reminded she should talk to Maralissa about Jesus, and she was just plain too scared.

"I've got an idea," Maralissa teased.

Jenna looked at her quickly. She was holding the address book up in both hands, waving it a bit and riffling its pages.

"I do too," Jenna quavered, suddenly certain she again knew what Maralissa meant.

A smile spread over Maralissa's face, and she held out the book to Jenna.

"First, the date, I think," Maralissa dictated playfully. "On Peggy Carver's letter. Today's date and our initials, stating that we succeeded in the Address Book Adventure."

"So the next people will know," Jenna still quavered, looking squarely at Maralissa, "that the adventure's been completed."

Maralissa held her gaze. "Exactly."

Sherry hitched herself closer to them on the sand, and they passed the book around and initialed the Peggy Carver pages in silence.

"Now," Jenna said, eyes again fastened on Maralissa, "a blank page?"

Maralissa let only a slight smile touch her lips. Her eyes sparkled.

Jenna paged through the book. There had to be a blank page. There was.

"This is what the first two sentences will read." Jenna's quaver was gone. "Hi, we're Sherry, Jenna, and Maralissa. Welcome to the Address Book Adventure."

❧

"That looked like quite a project you three had going on Maralissa's beach," Mom said to Jenna as they sorted dirty clothes in the basement laundry room. "No, I wasn't spying from the deck with a telescope." Mom laughed at the look Jenna gave her. "I was exploring Mixed-Up Forest with Ben and Tyler. Were you guys digging for treasure or what?"

Amazed, Jenna grabbed a shirt up to her face to hide her expression. She squinted in case her eyebrows should try to jump into her hairline.

"That's a pretty red ring."

Jenna lowered the shirt. "Mom, it has to stay a secret."

"Okay."

"You wouldn't want Maria to know what we did." Jenna hardly dared speak aloud. "She'd have a fit."

"By all means, let's avoid that," Mom said

dryly. She added detergent to the washer and pulled out the button that started water rushing into it.

Jenna was glad for the noise. If she couldn't talk to Mom above the racket, maybe she could forget about addresses and homes and Heaven and Maralissa and Jesus.

But it would be a wasted opportunity. Dad, David, and Peter hadn't come back from home yet. Lia and Sherry were watching Maria, Ben, and Tyler. Cara was off pouting somewhere because she was neither a little kid nor a big kid, and Grandma—Grandma was probably in her room. Jenna was alone with Mom, and there'd be no better time to talk.

"Mom?" She drew Mom into the mud room across from the laundry. The sound of rushing water receded a bit. Breathing a swift prayer that Melly would forgive her, she asked, "Did Grandpa go to Hell?"

Shock crossed Mom's face, and her blue eyes popped open. "Oh, Jenna, have you been worried about that?"

"Well, sure."

"Let's sit." Mom motioned toward a bench against the wall of the mud room. "You're wondering because we prayed for Grandma and Grandpa to become Christians?"

"Well, did he accept Jesus?"

Mom sighed and leaned her head back against the paneled wall. "Not that we know of."

"Well, isn't it true that we have to have Jesus to go to Heaven? I mean, do we really, really believe that?"

Mom turned to her, and her face lost all its uncertainty. "Yes, Jenna. I really, really believe that."

"And do the people who don't go to Heaven go to Hell?"

Mom's eyes closed briefly as she nodded. "Yes, they do."

"Well, then?" Jenna shrilled.

Head still leaning back, Mom seemed to be studying the ceiling. "God looks on the heart," she began. "We know what people think or feel or decide only if they do something to show us. But God can read exactly what's inside. So if Grandpa accepted Jesus, inside himself without telling anyone, before he died, he is in Heaven."

Jenna folded her arms across her chest and stuck her legs out straight. It sounded like a cop-out to her. "Adults don't talk about this stuff, do they? Did you and Uncle Bob talk about how your dad might have gone to Hell? Or did you and Dad?" She looked at Mom.

Mom gazed straight ahead at some clothes hanging on coat hooks on the opposite wall. "No, we didn't."

"So even though you believe in Hell, you pretend everybody goes to Heaven? Is that why everybody's acting normal, like nothing ever happened?" Jenna inhaled noisily. "But if Hell is real and it's really so horrible, how can we just keep going on like normal and laugh and have fun and everything? It's because we just forget about Hell, and we don't really care, right? Because if we talk about it, adults will freak out and not know what to say."

Mom was quiet for a while, and Jenna listened to the washer splish-splash the clothes. "Well, I don't think I'm freaked out," Mom finally said. "But it's true I'm not sure what to say to you. If I tell you no one's pretending, you probably won't believe me. I'm just trying to take in the way you feel."

"If Hell is real," Jenna said, "then don't we have to tell people not to go there?" Her heart began to pound in time with the washer. "But I can't do that. I can't tell people they have to be Christians or they won't go to Heaven. Kids would laugh their heads off. And adults will think I'm just a kid from a nutty church or a crazy family."

"Witnessing isn't easy," said Mom.

"I don't *like* this." Jenna stamped her feet on the floor like a short drumroll.

"Is there someone you feel you're supposed to witness to?"

"Maralissa," Jenna said miserably.

"Hmm," said Mom.

"And then there was Grandpa. Only that was so stupid. We ended up talking about how the sun looked like a peach that got born, and when I mentioned God to him, he pretty much thought it was silly—"

"Wait a minute, Jen—"

"And he *died* that morning!"

"Jenna." Mom held up her hand.

"So I don't think he was a Christian."

"Jenna, are you feeling guilty? Do you feel as if Grandpa might not be in Heaven because you had a talk with him that didn't go right?"

"Well—" She squirmed on the bench, and the bones in her upper back rubbed the wall. Maybe nobody liked to hear their fears talked about in plain words. Words, words. "I'm not sure."

"Honey, people have shared the gospel with Grandpa several times in his life. With Grandma, too. They thought Dad and I had joined a cult."

"You mean—a weird religion?"

"A group that teaches error about Jesus or the Bible," Mom said. "Uncle Bob tried to talk to them too when he became a Christian. They told him they felt okay about God and that everyone should keep their beliefs to themselves. And you remember how we've always prayed for Grandma and Grandpa."

Jenna nodded and came out of her slouch a bit.

"And you say you actually did mention God to Grandpa?"

"I said—I said something about God showing us part of Himself in each part of nature."

"You did?" Mom sat up perfectly straight. "Well, that's terrific, Jenna. You know, if the Lord wanted to speak to Grandpa one last time—" She faltered a bit. "Then letting him hear something about God and nature was the ideal way. Grandpa loved nature." She paused. "Far from saying the wrong thing, Jenna, I think God *used* you."

"Really?"

"Really. But remember something. We witness to people, but it's not the words we say that save them. Jesus is the only Savior, and each of us has to make our own decision for or against Him. Do you know the parable of the sower?"

Jenna nodded. She remembered this story Jesus had told because she had just read it in Luke. The story said words were like seeds, and different people were like shallow soil or rocky soil or thorny soil, or maybe good soil. The seeds could only grow in the good soil, and that was like saying the words were only remembered by the people who really paid attention to them. The rocky or thorny or shallow people never heard the words, or ignored them, or forgot them. They didn't keep the words, and the words could not keep them.

"You mustn't feel guilty about Grandpa. Sad or sorry or confused—maybe we have reason for all of those. But not guilt, honey. You did witness to Grandpa. You shared with him something you believe about God. What Grandpa chose is not your responsibility."

"Okay."

The washer had paused in its cycle. It suddenly jumped to life again as water began rushing out of it.

"Now, about Maralissa."

Maralissa! For a while Jenna had almost forgotten her.

"Sharing your faith with her may be just the right thing to do," Mom said. "It may be that right now you're earning the right."

"What?" Jenna was leaning forward on the bench now, and she looked at Mom.

"You're becoming friends. With friends we often find the right times to talk about personal things or touchy things," Mom explained. "If Maralissa enjoys your company and already knows you care about her, she will probably listen respectfully to you. That's what I mean by *earning the right* to talk about it."

"But Grandma and Grandpa didn't listen to you."

"Oh, they listened. They just didn't accept it. There are no guarantees, hon."

The washer clunked off just in time to make room for a new noise.

"Mom!" came Ben's muffled voice from upstairs. Overhead, the door crashed open. "Mom! I'm tired of Lia and Sherry."

"Honestly, Mom, I thought you were just throwing in a load of wash," Lia called. "Is the washer broken? Did you have to beat the clothes on a rock?"

The washer answered with a new clunk and a torrent of rinse water.

Mom jumped off the bench, an almost-wicked smile on her face. "Praise the Lord, it's healed!" she yelled toward the basement stairs. "Toss that old washboard in the corner, Jenna, and let's load up the automatic!"

In spite of herself, Jenna laughed.

"Mom, will you please just come up?" Lia pleaded.

"Dad's home!" Maria shouted.

"What's a washboard?" Jenna whispered loudly to Mom.

Mom smiled. "We'll have to have that talk another day."

❧ 11 ❧

The Storm

ON TUESDAY AFTERNOON THE SUN ruled the sky, stretching its rays as if to force out even the blue.

"It's really great that you found three rings that were all new colors," Jenna told Maralissa as they strolled down the public beach south of Bluerose Cottage. The two of them, with Sherry, had buried the new rings that morning. Pink, purple, and aqua, the rings clinked into the new baby food jar with a new note, and that went into the treasure chest and into a new twelve-inch hole on Maralissa's beach.

"I'm glad I did too," Maralissa answered. "Maybe the people who solve our adventure can buy red, blue, and green ones again for the adventure *they* write. Do you think it's getting windier?"

Jenna shrugged. It was always windy on the water. "If yellow rays of sun shine across blue sky, why doesn't the whole thing turn green?"

Maralissa laughed. "I don't know."

"The sun is queen of the sky today." Jenna threw some bravado into her voice and began to kick her legs out in front of her as she walked. She would need to work up courage to talk about the Lord. The wind brushed her and curled around her like a cat.

"There's your answer then," said Maralissa.

"Huh?"

"If the sun is queen, the sky has to surrender. Yellow wins, and blue backs off. No green. Green is blending."

"Or fighting?"

"Green is a tie," said Maralissa.

Jenna suddenly noticed the light had faded. She looked up and saw a fleet of marbled, sooty clouds sailing in. The wind rushed hard, shoving all her hair to the left side of her head, and this time it didn't let up. "Look!" she cried, pointing to the southwest where huge, dirty cauliflower clouds spilled over the trees.

"We'd better hurry," Maralissa shouted, turning back toward Bluerose Cottage as the first cold drops began to hit. "The queen has been dethroned."

In minutes they were drenched. Thunder that had begun grumbling like a car going over railroad tracks quickly began cracking and booming.

Lightning that looked like road maps blinked in the sky.

"Come away from the water, Jenna!" Maralissa, panting, grabbed her hand, and they struggled away from the shore. Now they were running at a right angle to the rain, which slashed them like sheets of liquid steel. Maralissa tripped and sprawled flat. Hail began to pelt them.

"Maralissa!" Jenna jerked at her arm, and Maralissa spun her legs trying to make the rest of herself follow. *Yes, adults can fall, Melly.* Maralissa gained her feet and shot forward like a sprinter at the starting gun.

"Oh, Jenna, Jenna, I think we'd better lie down." Maralissa sounded suddenly, strangely calm.

"What?"

"Have you ever seen a tornado?"

Jenna's neck snapped back, and she looked up before the fear had time to hit her. The clouds had a tail. The whole body-and-tail thing bobbed above them like a lazy black wasp. With Maralissa, Jenna hit the soggy ground and covered her head. This was exactly what she wanted to do when lazy black wasps bumped along the ceiling in her classroom at school, but she couldn't do it there. She felt a crazy relief at being able to do it now.

"This'll have to do. There's no ditch here," Maralissa gasped.

"Will it get us?" Jenna's voice made its best quaver ever.

"It's ahead of us going northeast. If we wait here, it should move away from us."

"Toward Bluerose Cottage?" Jenna swallowed. "Toward Happy Hill House?"

"I hope not."

"Oh, Jesus, help my family," Jenna prayed. She pictured Mom and Sherry and the little kids, who had been swimming, dashing out of the lake as the storm hit. She pictured Dad circling the cottage calling through his cupped hands, *calling her name*, his words blown apart by the wind. "Oh, Jesus, tell them I'm okay!"

The sky raged. She pictured Dad trying to talk Grandma down to the basement. She pictured Grandma dragging her dust-mop-slippered heels and wailing, "Nothing's going to happen. I want to stay in my room. Leave me alone."

"Jesus, don't let Grandma die in a tornado. She doesn't know You!"

She pictured the tornado curling around the tall honey-bronze house, pulling the roof to a point as if it were a tepee, and she pictured panes and sheets of glass exploding and spinning into the wind.

"Oh, Lord, please keep them safe."

Jenna turned herself out of a puddle and felt how thoroughly wet she was. "Is it raining slower?"

"I'm not sure I can get up." Maralissa rolled over with difficulty and gazed at the sky. Carefully, they maneuvered themselves and looked to the northeast, the southwest, and every other direction overhead.

"Thank You, Jesus," said Jenna. The funnel cloud was gone. "If it had blown up our houses, we'd know, right?"

"We'd know." Maralissa panted as if she were still running. "I'm not sure I can get up."

"Are you hurt?"

"No, no. Just really tired. Tell me something, Jenna. When you prayed, you said to—you said to Jesus that your Grandma doesn't *know* Him. What do you mean?"

Jenna had propped herself up on her elbows, meaning to sit. Now she quickly lay flat again so that Maralissa couldn't see her face. She made a splashing sound, and water soaked her scalp.

"I mean, who claims to *know* Him? I don't mean to embarrass you about your prayer. It was really nice that you prayed. But was there a reason you used that word?"

Jenna gazed up at the greenish-gray world. She grasped a word. "Spiritual."

"Spiritual what?"

"Knowing Jesus is spiritual. After you tell Him you want Him to be Your Savior, you pray, and you read your Bible, and you get to know Him." Jenna's heart began to pound. Her words sounded kindergartenish.

Maralissa didn't answer for a minute. "Do you believe in Hell?" she finally asked.

Jenna snapped her head to the right to see Maralissa. Her cheek slapped a puddle. She shook herself to keep water out of her ear, or maybe it was the meaning of the words that made her quiver. "Yes." She swallowed. "I was afraid my Grandpa went there."

Maralissa met Jenna's eyes for a long moment. "You really do believe, don't you?"

"I think God answered my prayer." Jenna's teeth chattered. She broke their gaze.

"Could've been the storm just moving away." Maralissa sounded faraway herself.

"But that's how the answer would come."

Maralissa was quiet for so long Jenna thought she had fallen asleep. Her own shivering was continuous now, and she could only quiet her teeth by clenching them tight.

"Maralissa? The storm's over."

Maralissa roused herself. "We have to get you home. Your parents must be worried sick."

Although the thick cloud cover was growing brighter, their walk back to Bluerose Cottage was like a slow squishy stumble through the dark. Maralissa took Jenna's arm and frankly leaned on her. Jenna, scared, steered her through the field of ankle-grabbing weeds and finally between the clusters of pines into Maralissa's own back yard.

The sight there made Maralissa cry out. Her maple tree lay uprooted across her yard like a pulled tooth. Its branches had destroyed her vegetable garden in one big bite.

"My vegetables," she moaned.

"Oh, Maralissa, I'm sorry. But please just go in and rest now, okay?"

"Nothing else I can do right now." Maralissa managed a smile as they stopped at her door. "We've had enough adventure for a while, huh? Next time you come over, we'll just have tea—or grape juice—up in my loft."

"I can't wait," Jenna said. "I love lofts."

Pushing streaming hair from her face, Maralissa gave her the smile again. "I'm not surprised."

❧

"We won't have to worry about firewood," Grandma remarked listlessly, wandering through the house and peering out of windows.

Mixed-Up Forest really was mixed up now. Several trees lay like downed bowling pins. Others had snapped off and left bare wood showing, like gigantic broken pencils.

"It's firewood from Jesus!" Maria chirped to Grandma.

"Pfft." The small sound burst from Grandma. "If I need firewood, all Jesus has to do is send me your dad and an ax, and they're already here." Grandma crossed the girls' loft and ruffled Maria's hair, but Jenna heard how dry her voice sounded.

The next several days were heavy brother-and-sister watching days for the older Vander Giffins, because they were heavy cleanup days for Mom and Dad.

Mom and Dad hauled away not only the big wood chunks they could manage, but also the smaller branches and bouquets of leaves that covered everything. Often the whole family, except for Grandma, helped. Orange trucks crawled up Lake Road and chipped up logs with a high buzzing sound. Dad even made sure Maralissa's maple tree was taken care of. The work and the baby-sitting made tempers fray.

"Honestly, if Mom had all these kids, why do I have to watch them all the time?"

"David, don't leave me with stupid Jenna."

"Jenna, don't leave me with stupid Lia."

"Can't Grandma watch the kids? She just sits in her room. You don't think she's freaking out or anything, do you?"

Once when the complaining got too loud, Dad

disappeared into the cottage and came suddenly charging out in his swimming suit, the garden hose leaping after him and gushing full blast. "Who's hot under the collar here? David?" *Whoosh*. "Cara?" *Splat*. "Peter?" *Whoosh*.

"Dad's spraying us in our *clothes!*"

"More, Dad!"

"What?" roared Dad. "You mean the fire's not out yet?" *Splatter*.

They swam in the lake, smacked their lips over pitchers of lemonade, and once Jenna led a small band of them through a thinner Mixed-Up Forest for a grape juice tea party in Maralissa's loft.

Another day there was a knock on Grandma's cottage door. Jenna opened it casually, but when she saw her best friend standing there, she let out a shriek.

"Kate Schmidt! How did you get here!"

"How come *she* gets to have a friend here?"

"All we need is more girls!"

"We're renting a cottage two miles from here," Kate told Jenna. They cartwheeled down the beach in the sun, Kate's coppery hair flashing and her pearly teeth set in a gleaming smile. "My mom and dad are trying to decide how our family should spend vacations. If we all like the cottage, they might buy one."

Jenna grinned, knowing the word *vacation* had seldom crossed Kate's lips. Her father had always been so busy with his job that their family had never traveled, camped, fished, or done anything just for fun. They probably weren't even sure what they would enjoy. Jenna was just glad to see Kate's family together and happy again.

"You'll have to meet Maralissa," Jenna said. But when they scampered down to Bluerose Cottage and knocked on the door, Maralissa wasn't home.

In the evenings Lia took to telling Wendy stories in the loft. Lia allowed Mom, Sherry, and Maria to tie her hair back in a blue ribbon and dress her in a blue gown with a sash. Jenna thought she looked just like Wendy in the Peter Pan movie.

"The storm was a drama of nature." Lia stood before them, clasping her hands under her chin. "Written, directed, and performed by atmospheric forces on—on the vast stage that is our earth."

"Oh, pleeeeez," David groaned.

"Unleashing the power, the chaos, the destruction that can befall us all—and that no mother can order cleaned up."

David fell on the floor gagging, but Cara laughed. So did Jenna. This was a flashback to the Lia she remembered.

"The whole world is a stage! Do you realize?" Lia clutched at her hair, then turned slowly, arms

out. "All of life is drama. Do you see how impor-
tant—"

"You may think you're being real original, but
Shakespeare got there ahead of you," David said.
"In the 1500s he said, 'All the world's a stage.'"

Lia ignored him. "And we *missed* it. Our planet
has a literature of its own, and its language and
meaning are *lost* to us when we are closed up
behind gray dungeon storm cellar walls by those
who would hinder our education." Her voice fell
to a near whisper, and she lowered her chin onto
her still-clasped hands, eyes closed. Her blonde
hair fell forward as if to close the curtain on the
performance.

"What's she talkin' about?" Peter looked
around for anyone who might clue him in.

"I want a real story, a Peter Pan story," Ben
whined.

"That was beautiful." Cara sighed.

"It stunk totally," said David.

Jenna wondered why Grandpa hadn't asked
Lia for words. Then she wondered what part of
Himself God had shown them in the storm. Was
He mad? Mad at her? Was He showing them just
how furious and devastating His anger—and
Hell—could be?

❦ **12** ❦

Catastrophe

JULY SLIPPED INTO AUGUST WITHOUT Jenna's knowing it, and soon the first week was gone. Longing to visit Maralissa and Bluerose Cottage, she zigzagged through Mixed-Up Forest and down to Maralissa's door. The door swung open after one knock.

"Hi, M—" Jenna's exuberant greeting died on her lips.

Maralissa had aged at least twenty years, maybe thirty or forty—once people got that old, who could tell? Her hair had been cut, and silver strands draped it like tinsel. She had gained weight. No—the Princess Maralissa had been turned into a hag by an evil witch who was jealous of her beauty. At least that's what Maria would have said.

"May I help you?"

The woman's voice too was Maralissa's, but like the rest of her, it was old and tired.

"Maralissa?" Jenna whispered. She tried to speak louder. "I mean—I'm looking for Maralissa."

The woman was still holding onto the door, and she swung it all the way back. The room behind her was an obstacle course of cardboard boxes and open drawers.

"Maralissa," said the old Maralissa woman.

"She lives here?" Panic began to roll up from Jenna's middle. Had she interrupted a burglary? But a look-alike burglar didn't make sense.

"You really called her that?"

Jenna's breathing broke away from her control and jerked up and down. She almost yelled, *What have you done with her?* But she settled into her quavery voice and asked, "Who are you?"

"I'm Mrs. Rosencranz. I'm her mother."

Her mother. Of course. "Is Maralissa home?"

Mrs. Rosencranz looked over her shoulder at the boxes. Then she craned her neck to see past Jenna, as if checking to see who else might be around before looking at her again. "You would be Jenna."

She nodded.

"Jenna, I'm sorry to tell you this, but your Maralissa died Tuesday night."

"What?" No. People couldn't keep popping off the face of the earth like this.

"I'm sorry she didn't tell you she was ill."

Maria's voice rang in her mind. *I want to see when the magic fairies come to bring her to the castle.*

"Did she attract a whole bunch of children here?" Mrs. Rosencranz shuffled back to the boxes, tossed some books into one, and slammed on a cover. "Or did they think she was odd?"

"I—well—," Jenna burbled. It was too hard a question, and she could hardly hear. A tornado in her brain was sucking up the words.

"Awfully irresponsible of Mary Ann to invent a new person, make new friends, and then leave *them* too. Don't suppose she thought how you would feel. Always had some idea she was some kind of princess." Mrs. Rosencranz slammed a tiny drawer in Maralissa's desk and sighed. "Then again, it was the end of her life. If she wanted to live a fairy tale in the north woods . . ."

Some words had made it through the whirling in Jenna's head. "Who's Mary Ann?"

Mrs. Rosencranz looked stricken. "Oh, I shouldn't have. It's like bursting your bubble or something. On the other hand, why should she get away with it?" The woman's voice roughened, and she kicked at a pile of papers. "I didn't even know what she was calling herself till I saw the name written down. Your name's here too someplace. That's how I knew it." She looked up. "Unless that's made up too?"

Dazed, Jenna shook her head. "Her name's Mary Ann?"

"Mary Ann Rosencranz. My daughter." Mrs. Rosencranz's mouth snapped shut. The wrinkles of pain on her face made her look both young and old.

The whirlwind in Jenna's head spun so fast it began to wail like the electric mixer. "Where's Maralissa?"

"It's true," came the soft words. "She died."

"No!"

"I'm so sorry, Jenna."

"What did she die of?"

"A type of leukemia."

"No!"

"I'll go home with you, explain to your parents . . ." Mrs. Rosencranz's voice was fading, fading beyond the siren in Jenna's mind.

"She can't be dead!" She'd scream her throat out, her brains out, her insides out. Mrs. Rosencranz would disappear, and it wouldn't be true.

"I'm so sorry."

"When's the funeral?"

"It was yesterday, at home in Peshtigo."

"No! I don't believe she's dead!"

"I'm so sorry."

"Is her grave in Peshtigo? I want to see it!"

138

"It was her wish to be cremated and have her ashes sprinkled over the lake."

"No! What have you done with her?"

Only Maralissa could answer the questions churning inside her, but she couldn't get through this awful, old, fake Maralissa to find her. And she couldn't listen anymore to these lies that just might twist into truth if she didn't get away.

Jerking back from Mrs. Rosencranz, scraping her knuckles on the stone archway, Jenna stumbled back to her grandmother's cottage.

It seemed everyone was in the great room.

"Jenna, comb your hair. You look like you just escaped from the zoo," Lia said.

"Are you your sister's keeper?"

"Jenna, what's—"

Jenna stamped to a halt and plopped her hands on her hips in a gesture that outdid Lia. "I will never, never ever take care of the little kids again," she roared at her astonished family. "I wouldn't be able to keep 'em alive!"

Finally exploding into tears, wondering why she had ever come in here, she charged down the basement stairs, through the mud room, out the garage, down to the shore, all the way out on the pier.

"I hate you!" she screamed at the lake, the wave-frosted, sparkly lake that layered bluer,

bluer, bluer to the horizon and rippled with life and had Maralissa's ashes in it. "Traitor!"

Of course, the water paid no attention. It only lapped its rustling, liquidy sounds, and she stayed only because her body had to take up space somewhere.

It was a good stretch of time before Dad's careful footsteps sounded on the wooden planks. They stopped halfway out. "Jenna, Mrs. Rosencranz called. She's very concerned."

"Did you know, Dad? Did you know Maralissa was dead?"

"No. We didn't."

Jenna exhaled. She couldn't have borne it if she'd been left in the dark just because she was a kid.

"I'm sorry, Jenna."

"That's what everybody keeps saying." The anger was back in her voice. "It doesn't help."

"Well, when you come right down to it, we can't help death. It happens."

"Why didn't she tell me?" Jenna stared straight out at the water.

"Well, suppose she had. Would you have had as much fun this summer? Would your times together have been happy, or maybe awkward and sad instead?"

Jenna didn't answer.

"From what Mrs. Rosencranz told us,

Maralissa wanted one last summer to live as if she wasn't sick. She wanted to be among people who didn't know because then they wouldn't treat her differently."

Jenna hoped he'd tell her more, but she couldn't ask.

"I don't think her mother agreed with her decision, and it made her feel awful to think you got hurt."

Jenna pulled her spine even straighter than it was. She didn't want to be a child who needed to be shielded. If adults could take the pain, so could she. She turned to Dad. The wind was rising, and his curly blond hair blew away from his face. Jenna's back was to the breeze, and her question would carry to Dad loudly and clearly.

"Where's Maralissa, Dad?"

Their eyes locked.

Dad's words were as careful as a rescuer creeping onto thin ice. "Did she know the Lord?"

A phrase of Mom's came to her. "Not that I know of."

They stared.

"You're not going to come out and tell me she's in Hell, are you?"

Dad's head shook in the same careful way. "No, I'm not."

"Why?" She heard the agony in her own voice.

"Because Hell is the end of hope. Because,

thank God, here on earth we see and know so little." Dad took a step closer. "Some people give up on their faith when a tragedy happens, but this is the very time it can kick into high gear. Jenna, God loves *everybody* more than you or I can love *anybody*. How must *He* feel when someone is lost?"

Jenna stared at Dad's kneecaps.

"He shares our grief. Another thing—if we know we belong to the Lord, then we understand we don't belong to ourselves. And we don't belong to the person who died. We have to live for God because we answer to Him. That's why giving up our whole lives to endless grief is wrong. Don't get *me* wrong." Dad's arm shot out, his palm flat. "Grief is healthy and necessary. We may always miss the person. But we go on."

Jenna decided to get the focus off herself. "Is Grandma going to go on?" She looked at his face again, the sun rounding the top of the sky and making her squint.

He nodded. "It's awfully early for Grandma yet. She lived with Grandpa thirty-eight years. After the funeral is over, after the sympathy cards stop coming, after a couple of weeks pass, and the person is still gone, it begins to sink in that you're really going to have to live without him. That's what's happening to Grandma. That's why we're staying with her."

Thirty-eight years. That much time was beyond understanding.

"Jenna."

She looked at Dad.

"About—Hell. *We don't know* who's there. But we hold on to the assurance that our Christian friends aren't there. And we hope the others we know aren't there because we need that hope." He paused. "I don't think I could face *knowing* someone I love won't be in Heaven until I'm there myself and can share Christ's pain—and His comfort."

Jenna nodded.

"Would you let me pray with you?"

Jenna nodded again. She sat cross-legged in the middle of the pier, letting the planks dig into her skin, so that Dad would join her there. She was not ready to let her feet dangle in the lake.

❧ 13 ❧

Discovery

IT WAS STRANGE TO JENNA THAT Bluerose Cottage outlived Maralissa. Some days she tried to get a glimpse of it to see if it was still standing. Other days, riding past it on Lake Road, she turned her face away.

Maybe the presence of Mrs. Rosencranz kept the little house from falling down. She knew Mrs. Rosencranz was still there because one morning the woman knocked at Grandma's door and asked to see Jenna.

"Thought you might like something to remember her by. I found this with some of her things." Mrs. Rosencranz's palm stretched in front of Jenna. There lay Maralissa's blue ring.

Jenna tucked her hands into the back waistband of her shorts.

"You can take it, dear. She didn't have much, but she'd want you to have something."

Jenna didn't want it. But she'd been rude

enough to Mrs. Rosencranz already, and she was standing in the great room with some of her family, including Mom, looking on.

"Thank you."

As soon as Mrs. Rosencranz left, Jenna took the ring outside, still carrying it in her palm. She would not put it on her finger. Maralissa would not have given her this ring. Maralissa would have worn it to her funeral. Maybe the funeral home people had taken it off her finger. They shouldn't have.

Jenna milled around awhile, a few paces up the lumpy graveled Lake Road, a few turns through the cool trees. She wanted to make sure her family hadn't followed her. She wanted some time to hold the ring.

Eventually she made her way to the sand. The wooden planks muffled her steps as she walked to the end of the pier.

"I'm not throwing it away," she told Maralissa or the lake—she wasn't sure which. "It's just that if you don't have it anymore, it's like you dropped out of the game. I know you didn't. That's why your ring has to be where you are."

She wondered if she could do it. She should get David, who was an all-around athlete, or Cara, who was good at baseball. But it was up to her.

"Here, Maralissa. Catch." She wound her arm up as best she could and flung the ring into the sunlight. Spinning, it caught the rays and flashed once, twice, before diving with a soundless blip into the water.

❦

Another week floated by. The family went outside when the sun shone, came in when it rained. Grandma came out of her room a few times, put off her dust-mop slippers, and put on cushioned white walking shoes.

Dad spent time in the basement running some tools. Jenna was quiet, and no one, not even David, Lia, and Sherry, who got stuck with it, asked her to baby-sit.

That thoughtfulness was the very thing that made her think maybe, just maybe, she could baby-sit again some day.

"Jenna."

She was walking down the hill near the south bend of Mixed-Up Forest when she heard Maralissa's voice. She jerked her head up so fast her neck cracked.

"Didn't mean to startle you." It was Mrs. Rosencranz, of course. "Can't believe I didn't find this before now. Honey, Mary Ann—*Maralissa*—left you this." She held out a white envelope. It was thick and had her name written on the front. A strange pang struck her. How odd to see the handwriting of a dead person.

"Thank you." She took the envelope, came alive, filled up with sudden eagerness to tear it open. Or should she be scared? Would it hint of something she didn't want to know?

Seeing her agitation, Mrs. Rosencranz turned to leave. "Thank you," she said then, over her shoulder. "Good that Maralissa had a friend. *Mary Ann* had lots of friends, you understand, but Maralissa—well, she only lived one summer. You were her best friend. Know what I mean?"

Jenna found her voice. "Yes. She would know what you mean too."

A little thrill passed over Mrs. Rosencranz's face. "Would she? You really think she would? That phrase is music to my ears. Thank you, Jenna. Just about made my day."

Mrs. Rosencranz turned and bustled off. Jenna stared after her for a long time, before slipping between the trees and tearing the envelope open.

Dear Jenna,

If you're reading this, you know I have died. I'm truly sorry for the shock this will cause you. I've had leukemia for a long time, and I've had all the treatments. It went away twice, even long enough for my hair to grow back some, but when the cancer came back again, I knew my chances were really bad. I was tired of the treatments, and I wanted to live the time I had left without everybody knowing I had cancer. I hope you can understand a little.

That was why I wasn't very friendly when we first met. I knew you'd just lost your grandpa, and I was afraid to hurt you. But if I snubbed you, I'd hurt you too, and I'd be living like a cancer victim instead of a normal person. So we had to take the risk and be friends. Love and friendship will mean pain sometimes. We hate it when it happens, but we can't avoid it and really live.

Your sister's talk about fairy tales, Rapunzel, and everything, and asking me point blank if my name was Maralissa really freaked me out. I've always dreamed of living the life I lived this summer, and I asked myself if I was really wishing to live a fairy-tale life, and why. Think about what's in a fairy tale: good and evil, magic help for both sides, beauty, romance, tragedy—and then evil is vanquished, and there's happily ever after. We're fascinated with fairy tales because we're looking for Heaven!

I found a Bible among my books, and since the storm I've spent most of my time with it. I laughed when I read in Luke that if we won't receive the Kingdom of God like a child, we won't enter it. If I'm living a fairy tale, I must be something like a child, right? And in Revelation I read that to those who overcome evil Jesus will give a new name known only to them. I wondered if maybe I jumped the gun trying to give a new name to myself.

I read about knowing and seeing only a little here on earth, and knowing and seeing so much more in Heaven. I read about all of Heaven rejoicing when one sinner repents.

I began to see the wonderful life God wants to give me in Heaven and how I had tried to give it to myself here on earth. That's what really made me get down on my knees and ask Jesus to forgive me. After that, I wanted to read the Bible even more.

You were right, Jenna! After you take Him as your Savior, you pray, and read your Bible, and you feel like you get to know Him. A little, anyway, because I won't have long.

In Heaven we're going to have a home, Jenna. Better than Bluerose Cottage! Better than Happy Hill House!

And that's no fairy tale.

See you there.

With love,
Maralissa Rose
(Mary Ann Rosencranz)

Jenna's heart thudded. She flopped down on her back and watched the leaves wave wildly and cheer in leaf language overhead. She jumped up, grabbed the pages, and flew over ruts, grass, blacktop, boulders, up the wooden steps.

"Mom, Dad!" She sailed into the great room. "She went to Heaven! She . . . Where's Mom and Dad? Mom, Dad!"

"Honestly, Jenna, you'd think you could help with lunch or something. I mean, maybe you could put one little fork on the table."

"Hey, I thought she was the one who didn't like noise. Keep it down, will ya?"

Someone clumped up from the basement. "Jenna?" Dad asked, "What's the matter? You okay?"

"What's all the noise about?" Mom appeared from the direction of the first-floor bedrooms with Tyler and his toothbrushes in tow.

"Look!" Jenna thrust the letter at them. "She went to Heaven! She's there!"

"Heaven for real?" asked Maria.

"Yeeees!" screeched Jenna.

Lia paused in her table-setting. "She was just too unreal to stay."

"Lia!"

"Sorreee." Lia put her hands up defensively. "I mean, hey, that's great."

"Mom, listen." Jenna's voice was as shaky as a sheep's baa.

"Idea time," announced Cara.

"Does it really say in the Bible that all rejoice in Heaven when one sinner repents?"

"Yes, it does," Dad said.

"And this—all this—is really real, right?" Jenna looked from one parent to the other, noticing her own panting for the first time. She swiped the back of her hand across her forehead.

Mom and Dad laughed.

"Yes, it's really real. Right." Mom stressed all her *R*s.

"Really, really real," kids repeated.

"Right."

"For real."

"Okay, then, we have to have a party," Jenna said. "I mean, *may* we have a party? A Maralissa's-in-Heaven party? Please? We could have it tonight."

"Cool!"

"Yeah, a party!"

"I'll make the dessert," Jenna said.

Mom and Dad looked at each other. Dad wore a maybe-we-should look, and Mom smiled a silly smile.

"It might be just the thing," said Mom. She flashed some kind of eyebrow signal at Dad. "Just the thing indeed."

Grandma did not object to a party. "Well, sure." She laughed a bit self-consciously when Mom carefully told her what the occasion was. "We can remember Stan too, after all."

The weather was as glorious as the celebration. A dome of china-blue sky rode above them, holding fat, white clouds with sharp cookie-cutter edges. The breeze was no more than a gentle massage on the skin, and waves lapped and comforted the sand smooth.

For supper there was barbecued chicken and a corn roast in special honor of Maralissa. Lemonade and soda flowed freely. After Jenna's angel food cake with vanilla custard filling and white chocolate frosting, even the children could hardly move.

"But I must ask you to take a walk up the driveway," Dad told everyone. "There's a little something that needs to be said."

At the top of Grandma's driveway, right where it met Lake Road, Jenna saw that a black pole had been stuck into the ground. A pretty light fixture sat on its top. A small arm stretched out below that, and the arm had two hooks.

"According to the wishes of the owner of this residence," Dad extended his arm toward Grandma, "the time has come to bestow upon it a name. Ben Vander Giffin, you will please present the plaque."

Ben sashayed up to Dad holding something behind his back. Alarm crossed his face as he juggled it, deciding which hand he'd use. Finally he brought it forward.

"Oohh," everyone said.

Dad held before them a curved wooden sign that read *Happy Hill House* in fancy lettering. A cluster of three pines decorated its right edge.

"Ma'am?" Dad handed the plaque to Grandma, who threaded the two holes along its top over the two hooks on the pole. The sign swayed ever so slightly, as if experimenting on its new swing.

"I present to you—Happy Hill House," Dad said to them all. "May it be a blessing to the Schellenburg family for many years to come."

"Yaaaaay," said Peter. Some began to applaud, others joined in, and they had a real clapping and cheering session before trooping back down the driveway.

Jenna hung back until the end, smiling at the sign and thanking God that Grandma could call it a happy house again, as Maralissa had said she would. Then she followed her family down the hill—to Happy Hill House.

❦ 14 ❦

Keeping Words

AND, AS MARALISSA HAD SAID THEY would, the neighbors left their cottages before the end of August.

Jenna's watch beeped at 6:05 A.M. on packing day. She found the lake breeze fresh and new that morning, blowing in just a hint of a chill, reminding her of the red-tinged and gold-edged leaves beginning to sneak into Mixed-Up Forest. She ran her hands through the sand, making a dry cushion for herself and feeling it conform to her body as she settled into it. She opened her journal.

The words she'd read to Grandpa were written there. In this ink, on these pages, they'd last as long as the book did. Some words lasted no longer. But other words, *keeping* words, were carried in people's hearts, maybe for all of their lives. Like the Bible, and Maralissa's letter, and Peggy Carver's address book waiting in the window seat to be found by future owners of Bluerose Cottage.

Maybe even like her words to Grandpa and Grandpa's to her. She remembered how some simple words she'd said seemed to mean so much to Mrs. Rosencranz. She remembered longer ago how she'd prayed for her turn to talk. It could be that her words to Grandpa had found a keeping place in his heart, the way seeds find a home in good soil.

Uncapping her pen, Jenna began to write.

After all, she thought, *even if I didn't know Maralissa was in Heaven, she'd still be there.*

That was such a big thought, she began to scrawl faster. But she looked up in time to see a fiery arc clear the surface of the lake as the sun began to rise.